Advance Reviews for Deadly Ransom

"Matt Davis is back—and that's bad news for the bad guys! Matt Davis, the former NYC homicide detective, nearly killed in the line of duty in Joe Perrone Jr.'s debut, *As the Twig is Bent*, thought he'd found peace and quiet as chief of a small, Upstate police department. But trouble has an uncanny way of finding him. It's kidnapping and arson this time around in Perrone's fifth Matt Davis mystery, *Deadly Ransom*," a must-read for his many fans."

—Tom Connor, co-author of the *New York Times* best-selling *Martha Stuart's Better Than You at Entertaining*.

*   *   *   *

"Generally I do not read serial novels, and I admit to fighting to keep preconceived prejudices at bay when I started this read. To my surprise, *Deadly Ransom* is a page turner, or in this day and age of eBooks, a page 'swiper.'

Author Joe Perrone Jr. cleverly presents his latest thriller in a psychophrenic storyline. Matt Davis, a former NYPD detective, now Chief of Police in Upstate Roscoe NY, is asked by an old friend to solve a kidnapping in Montana. Davis convinces his boss, the mayor, to allow him a long overdue vacation, and agrees to work on his own time. As the mystery in Montana plays out, back in Roscoe, an arsonist runs loose, keeping Matt's temporary substitute quite busy. The entire novel has the reader rooting for his replacement to solve the arson mystery so that Matt doesn't return to New York, having solved the Montana crime only to find an unresolved mess at home.

Among the things I like are the short chapters. As you read along, there is a comfortable certainty in knowing the action will shift when you reach the end of a chapter. The scene either shifts from protagonist to antagonist, or re-opens the action, either in Montana or Upstate New York.

Although part of a series, *Deadly Ransom* has a strong enough plot and character development to allow it to stand on its own. In fact, your curiosity might be piqued enough to return to the scene of the crime and work your way through the first four books in the series."

—**Greg Miller, Production Manager,** *Thomson Reuters;* **author of** *Springsteen—A Notion Deep Inside* **(2016-www.BossScribbler.com)**

*   *   *   *

"*Deadly Ransom* is just that, another Matt Davis mystery well worth the cover price. However, this time you get two Matt Davis cases for the price of one. Matt and former partner, Chris Freitag, are off to Montana—*not* to fish, but to rescue a kidnapped ranch hand named Shorty. While Matt's away, Roscoe is burning, as an arsonist terrorizes the countryside. Author Joe Perrone Jr. takes the reader on his typical twisted ride, this one from the Catskills to the big skies of Montana. The cast includes cowboys, Indians, an arsonist, and more three-dimensional characters.

In the end, it's Matt's good old common sense and his lifetime of experience that saves the day. *Deadly Ransom* is a welcome addition to the Matt Davis Mystery Series and will hold your attention right up to the conclusion."

—**Jim Krul, former director Catskill Fly Fishing Museum and Center, Livingston Manor, NY**

Deadly Ransom
A Matt Davis Mystery

by

Joe Perrone Jr.

Deadly Ransom: A Matt Davis Mystery
By Joe Perrone Jr.

Dedication

To my one and only granddaughter. You have been the light and inspiration for my keeping on. Without your spirit and its presence in my life, it is doubtful that this book would ever have been finished.

Other Books by Joe Perrone Jr.

Fiction

As the Twig is Bent: A Matt Davis Mystery
Opening Day: A Matt Davis Mystery
Twice Bitten: A Matt Davis Mystery
Broken Promises: A Matt Davis Mystery
Escaping Innocence: A Story of Awakening

Non-Fiction

A "Real" Man's Guide to Divorce (First, you bend over and . . .)

Gone Fishin' with Kids (How to Take Your Kid Fishing and Still be Friends) co-authored with Manny Luftglass

All of the above books, with the exception of *Gone Fishin'*, are available in e-book formats through Amazon.com and other e-book distributors, and in audio books through Audible.com.

All five works of fiction are available in large print. *As the Twig is Bent* is also available in Portuguese and Spanish. A German translation is currently being done, with its release scheduled for April or May.

Chapter 1

Beaverhead Valley, Southwestern Montana

The bull weighed more than thirteen hundred pounds and was named Tyrus, after the Hall of Fame baseball player, Ty Cobb. Like his namesake, Tyrus was a stud — and just as ornery as the legendary Georgia Peach, according to his owner, Clint Davidson. Tyrus was a classic example of a breed-grade Braunvieh bull, two years old and in his sexual prime. His only purpose in life was to provide regular quantities of high-priced semen sold to other ranches for purposes of artificial insemination, or "A.I." as it was referred to in ranching circles. The Davidsons had a dozen or so of the Braunviehs, but Tyrus was their number one producer.

Clint owned the Crooked Creek Cattle Ranch, a 13,500-acre spread that was bordered on its western flank by the Beaverhead River, a blue ribbon trout stream. Numerous tributaries, chock full of game fish, ran through the property. Clint and his wife had purchased the ranch two years earlier from Denyse Salmon, a widow whose late husband's family had owned the property for nearly a hundred and twenty five years. When Joe Salmon passed away after a massive stroke, and with no children as heirs, it was inevitable that Denyse give up the land. The Davidsons made a generous offer and a deal was struck.

The ranch's pastures held more than fourteen hundred head of Black Angus, including mother cows, bred half-blood Braunvieh/Angus Heifers, and some bulls.

Sixty-seven-year-old Clint watched as Shorty McMann led the single-purposed bull toward the waiting surrogate by a short rope attached to a nose ring. Shorty was anything but short; he was six feet-two and weighed two hundred pounds. He'd been tagged with the moniker while still a late-blooming teenager, and it had stuck. As part of the sale arrangements, Shorty had agreed to stay on as foreman for at least two years in order to assist the new owners. The arrangement had served both Clint and the ranch hand well, and it was assumed that Shorty would remain with the Davidsons until he chose to retire—if he ever did.

Now, a four-year-old cow was positioned in a capture chute, its hind end available to the task. The targeted bovine had been prepped by having its pubic hair trimmed and its private parts washed with a sterile solution (to prevent the bull from possibly contracting venereal disease in the event of an accidental penetration). All of this was done to facilitate the false mounting required to stimulate the bull and increase the count and motility of its sperm— the ultimate prize. Rather than depositing its semen into the cow, the bull's member would be guided by a lucky AI tech into an artificial vagina used to capture the five-or-so-milliliters of ejaculate.

The bull snorted, pawed the ground, and approached the cow. He was more than ready to perform. In less than a minute, the deed had been done, and Tyrus was led away from his uncaring partner for a well deserved, but brief respite.

A few minutes later, after the tech had finished emptying the capture vessel into a sterile container, Shorty said, "Okay, let's give him another shot at it." He steered Tyrus to a different cow by the nose ring, and in less than thirty seconds, the whole process was repeated. Finally, after a third "performance" with still another cow, Tyrus was led back to his corral—to rest and recuperate from the stressful event.

The cattle business had been good to the Salmon family. Two years prior, gross receipts had topped a half million dollars, a far cry from the hand-to-mouth existence Joe Salmon's ancestors had hacked out of the land when they first migrated West in 1891. Now, as Clint made his way back to the house on his palomino, he thought of all those who had gone before him and smiled. Of course none of the Salmons could have made a dime without the help of the hundreds of ranch hands who had served them so well down through the years. Of all the ranch hands whom Clint employed, none could hold a candle to Shorty, his foreman and, of late, his best friend. He often wondered what he would do without him.

Soon, he would learn just that.

Chapter 2

Roscoe, New York

Chief of Police Matt Davis had just finished going over the early morning wants and warrants on his computer, noting a bulletin regarding a barn burning over in Green County, when Nancy Cooper, his secretary, shouted to him from her office across the hall. "Hey, Matt, you've got a phone call!"

"Who is it?"

"He *says* he's Chris Freitag." (Chris had been Matt's partner back in the city, and was married to Rita Valdez, another member of Matt's homicide squad.)

"Hmmm . . . I wonder what he wants. "

"I don't know," replied Nancy. "I guess you'll just have to pick up line one and find out."

Matt grabbed the handset and shouted into the mouthpiece, "Is this the world famous New York homicide detective, Chris Freitag?"

"No," said the voice on the other end of the line, "It's Mayor DeBlasio. Who the hell did you *think* it was, you asshole?"

Some things never changed. Freitag was as feisty as ever. Just hearing his old friend and partner's voice was enough to make Matt smile. How long had it been anyway? *Christ, I haven't talked to him since the wedding.*

"So what's goin' on?" Matt asked. "What's happening in *Haus Freitag*? How's Rita?"

"Rita's just fine. And, before you ask, no, she's *not* pregnant."

"Too bad," said Matt. "I'm genuinely disappointed."

"Well *don't* be. You know how I feel about dogs, cats, and kids. They're just great—as long as they belong to someone else."

"So surprise me. What's going on?"

"Wel-l-l, I know this is going to sound crazy, but I need a favor . . . actually, somebody we both know needs a favor—a *big* one." The tone of Freitag's voice had changed from light-hearted to deadly serious.

"Who is it? Is it somebody from the precinct?"

"No, no. It's Ralph Gilly, the guy from the fishing ranch out in Montana. You remember Ralph, don't ya?"

"Yeah, of course. Jesus, what's it been, ten years since we were there?"

"At *least*," replied Chris.

"So what kind of favor does he need? Is he in some kind of trouble?"

"No . . . well . . . not exactly. It's a friend of his, a cattle rancher. He's got *big* problems."

"What kind of problems? And why's Ralph calling *you*?"

"It's a long story," sighed Chris, "but his friend really needs our help."

"*Our* help?"

"Yeah. *Both* of us. I can't just go out there by myself."

"Go where? *Montana*?"

"Yeah, Montana. Listen, have you got a few minutes?"

"For you? Of course. What about lunch? Why don't you come on up to Roscoe, and we'll go to Raimondo's. My treat."

"Hmmm, that's very tempting . . . and I'd love to, I really would, but I can't get away right now. Just listen to me for a minute, okay. This friend of Ralph's, his name is Clint, and he . . . "

Fifteen minutes later, after Chris had explained things, Matt hung up the phone. "Nancy! If anybody calls, take a message and tell them I'll call them back. I'm going over to see Harold."

Chapter 3

Montana

The previous day's semen collection had been a huge success, and Clint Davidson awoke refreshed after a full night's sleep, which, for a change, had not been interrupted once by his aging prostate.

He sat up in the king-sized bed, stretched his arms over his head, and turned to his left. But of course, his wife Harriet wasn't there. It had been a little over a year since the love of his life had succumbed to a sudden heart attack and died at the tender age of 60, but the habits learned over forty years of marriage hadn't died with her—at least not yet. Clint still slept on the left side of the bed, and probably always would. Harriet's side remained as neat as if it had just been made.

Bright sunshine peeked around the edges of the mini blinds that covered the two large windows on the eastern wall of the enormous bedroom, almost as if attempting to grow the flowers that adorned the wallpaper. Clint couldn't help but feel energized. He glanced over at the grandfather clock in the corner and noted it was seven already. *Jeez. Half the day's nearly gone.* He sighed and swiveled around to the edge of the bed, letting his long legs dangle over the side. He dropped down onto the hardwood floor, padded over to the leather recliner by the

TV, and retrieved his jeans and long-sleeved, western shirt from where he'd left them the night before.

Fifteen minutes later, after an ice cold shower (the only kind he ever took), he dressed for the day and clomped down the stairs in his cowboy boots, headed for the kitchen in the back of the house.

That's strange, he thought, as he made his way along the back corridor, he couldn't smell the coffee.

"Shorty?" he called out. "What happened to the coffee?"

Shorty was not only the ranch foreman, he was a hell of a cook. He lived in a small cottage behind the main house, and the first thing he did every morning was come over and brew a hot steaming pot of coffee, long before he ever peeled one potato, or fried one strip of bacon. It was a ritual. That's why Clint couldn't comprehend the absence of the familiar aroma — any more than he could understand why his ranch foreman was nowhere to be found.

Chapter 4

Roscoe, NY

Mayor Harold Swenson listened patiently as Matt explained the situation. When he was done, he asked, "How long would you be gone?"

"We've got ten-day, round-trip tickets. It might only take a few days, or it might take a week or more, but the bottom line is that I've got to go."

Harold frowned. It was an expression he wore more than any other. "I'm glad that you feel such an obligation to a complete stranger, but what about your obligation to Roscoe? It's the middle of the summer, for Christ's sake. What about us?"

"Look, Harold, you and I both know that I haven't taken a vacation since I became chief. Hell, what's it been, four years? Maybe longer. And I've *never* complained. Living here in Roscoe, being able to fly fish these great rivers is all I ever wanted, so I've got no problem with answering the call of duty. But this is something I really *need* to do."

Harold slid back and forth in his wheeled armchair, his eyes focused on the ceiling, as if searching for some divine guidance.

"What about jurisdiction out there? After all, you guys aren't licensed in Montana."

"No, you're right. And I've thought about that. We're *not* licensed in Montana. But basically the way it works is that we'll be acting as private investigators for a *private* citizen. We won't be constrained by the same limitations that apply to law enforcement. It's actually *better* in some ways."

"So, the town of Roscoe isn't involved at all," Harold said. "There's no liability to us at all. Is that correct?"

"Absolutely."

Harold let Matt's response register, then voiced his *real* objection. "Who's going to fill in for you? We've only got four officers—and *that* includes you."

All the while he'd been speaking, Harold had been pushing against the floor with his toes. Now, the back of the chair slammed into the wall behind him and he slid forward, almost onto the floor.

"Damn it, Matt," groused Harold. "We're in a tight spot."

Matt smiled.

"What's so damned funny?!"

"I'm sorry, Harold. It's the movie."

"What movie?" Harold was genuinely perplexed.

"Oh Brother, Where Art Thou? It's a line from the movie. George Clooney's character is always saying . . ."

It was obvious that Harold wasn't "getting it."

"Oh, forget about it," Mat laughed. "It was stupid."

"Yeah, just like this hare-brained idea of yours about going to Montana with your sidekick. What's his name? *Frytack*?"

"Frei*tag*."

"Whatever."

"Can I go, or not?"

"Fuck no, you can't go."

"Fine. Then I quit." Matt started to remove the badge from his tunic. "Get somebody else to write your damned parking tickets."

"Hang on," sputtered Harold. "Just hang on a damned minute. Jesus, Matt. You sure don't make it easy."

"It can't be helped."

"What if I *were* to let you go? How do you intend to pay for this?"

"That's my business. But I promise you it won't cost Roscoe a dime."

"I should hope not."

The sparring match was on. It didn't matter what it was that Matt requested from the town's chief executive; whether it was new phones (every officer now had a cell phone) or a box of paper clips, the level of combat was always the same. Harold just seemed to relish the fight — regardless of the outcome.

"Okay, okay. But you still haven't told me how you plan to replace yourself while you're gone."

Truth be told, Matt hadn't given any consideration to that part of the equation. As he had done all his life, he'd been faced with an emergency and dived into the water with all his clothes on. Harold had a point.

"Well?"

"I'm thinking."

"Well, when you've got an answer, we'll talk about it some more."

"Bill Patterson," said Matt.

"Who the *hell* is Bill Patterson?"

"He's the State Police Commander over at Troop C Barracks in Sidney."

"And *he's* going to take your place while you're gone? I don't think so."

God, Harold, thought Matt, *you're such an idiot.* "No, no, of course not," he explained. "But I can talk to him and see if they can cover our graveyard shift while I'm gone. They can bill us for the man hours, and I'll get the folks in Montana to pick up the tab."

"We can *do* that?"

"Why not? Little towns like ours do it all the time. Especially if an officer gets hurt on the job, or if someone has to go into the hospital, or something like that."

While Harold processed the information, Matt couldn't help imagining what was going through the mayor's mind. A consummate politician, he was undoubtedly trying to figure out some way he could take advantage of the situation.

"Okay," blurted out Harold. "You can go. But *only* if you can get the state guys to cover your ass. And when this is all over, I want you interviewed by the newspaper folks over in Monticello, so you can tell everybody about how you and *I* saved your buddy's ass in Montana — owing it all of course to the generosity of Trout Town USA."

Son of a bitch always has an angle.

"It's a deal," Matt conceded. "I'll get on it right away. And I promise you, Harold, you won't regret this . . . oh . . . and thanks."

"Don't thank me yet. If Bill Patterson thinks you're as crazy as I do, you won't be going anywhere."

Matt didn't need to hear any more negativity from the mayor. The door to Harold's office rattled loudly as he slammed it behind him.

Chapter 5

Montana

When Clint didn't find Shorty in the kitchen, his first thought was that the foreman had been out drinking the night before and had failed to set his alarm clock. It didn't happen often, but every once in a while Shorty became despondent and went on a little bender. Clint valued the man too much to make a stink over it. Montana could be a lonely place for a single fellow, something that Clint was beginning to understand only too well since losing Harriet.

First he checked the little two-room cottage that Shorty lived in, out behind the main house. There was a living room with a kitchen and dining area, a bedroom, and a tiny bath. Not much to look at from the outside, and only slightly nicer within. But to Shorty, it was home, and he kept it as clean as if it were an upscale garden apartment.

Clint knocked softly once, then twice on the weathered door, purely as a courtesy, just in case his foreman had a female visitor.

No answer.

He knocked again, this time hard enough to scrape his knuckles, and without waiting for a reply, pushed open the unlocked door and stuck his head inside. "Shorty?" he whispered, "are you in there?"

Nothing.

Clint stepped inside the combination front room, wiping his feet on the rubber welcome mat. All the lights were out, and there was no sign of Shorty.

That's strange, he thought. *He must've really tied one on last night.*

He walked over to the bedroom door and tapped on it softly. "Shorty," he laughed, "come on, man, it's time to get up. You know I can't start my day without some coffee."

Still no answer.

"Well, *this* is bullshit," said Clint, as he pushed open the bedroom door. He was no longer amused; he was pissed. "Shorty McMann, get your lazy ass up and . . ."

The room was empty.

"What the hell?" Clint stood there, totally perplexed, his hands on his hips. Not only was Shorty missing, the bed was unmade and the little milk glass lamp that usually sat atop the night table was on the floor, its white glass base shattered.

The corral, thought Clint. *That must be it.*

Certain that he'd find Shorty there, he headed out of the cabin, closing the front door behind him. The morning was particularly calm, with not a hint of wind, and gave no indication of the trouble on the horizon.

Gonna be a hot one.

He walked quickly toward the corral.

He hadn't been particularly upset at finding the coffee not yet made; he was mostly curious. But something had precluded Shorty from performing his most vital early morning task, and Clint was anxious to know what it was.

He certainly wasn't angry. Far from it. Nothing Shorty had ever done was enough to raise Clint's ire. It was more a sense of concern rather than disapproval that he was feeling. Was there a problem with the livestock? A wolf attack, perhaps, or worse yet, maybe a grizzly. What if something had happened to Shorty? A heart attack maybe. He pictured his friend lying in the dust of the corral and quickened his pace.

As he walked, he passed several enclosures, most of them used for branding, breeding, and other assorted purposes. There were a dozen or so pole barns, designed to provide shelter for the animals during the harshest part of the winter, and an equestrienne-style barn to house the horses his ranch hands used. Then, there was one special barn designated for his prize bulls. Outside that building was a small corral. When Clint arrived at the enclosure, Shorty was nowhere to be seen. The other wranglers were no doubt out on the range, their day already two hours old. The corral was empty. Clint squinted and peered through the bright rays of the early morning sun, trying to catch a glimpse of Tyrus.

That's strange. Where's Tyrus?

Clint took great pleasure every morning at seeing his prize bull standing alone in the corral, his massive presence a symbol of all that Clint and Harriet had just begun to build—up until she died.

Clint put the first two fingers of his right hand in his mouth and whistled loudly. "Tyrus! Where are you boy?"

Nothing.

I guess he's in the barn.

Unlike the other cattle that roamed the pastures day and night, Tyrus and the other bulls enjoyed the comfort of their own corrals and the protection of a small barn allocated exclusively for that purpose. Clint saw that the barn door, which opened to the corral, was closed.

Must be inside.

As he approached the massive sliding door, he noticed there was a six-inch gap between the edge of the door and the frame. The padlock was undone and hanging on its hasp.

"Shorty!" called Clint. "Are you in there?"

No answer.

Assuming Tyrus was inside the barn, he ought to be locked within his metal stall. Clint knew from personal experience that a little precaution went a long way in preventing accidents, so he switched on the bank of lights that illuminated the interior of the barn. He peered inside, but his eyes could detect no movement whatsoever. However, they did observe that the door to the bull's stall was wide open.

"What the hell?" he murmured.

Clint whistled loudly. "Tyrus! Hey, boy! Where's my Tyrus?"

Nothing.

He swiveled his head left and right, searching for any sign of his prize angus, as he made his way cautiously to the open stall. It was empty; at least that's what it appeared to be at first glance.

Then Clint looked down and saw the bull.

It was lying on the floor — dead. A large pool of blood, partially coagulated, surrounded the body. His massive throat had been slit. There was a bundle lying near the bull's head, and Clint bent down and picked it up. Newspaper had been wrapped around something soft and damp — and fairly heavy. Attached to the newspaper was a note. The message it contained made Clint's blood run cold.

Chapter 6

Roscoe, NY

Matt had called Bill Patterson over in Sidney just five minutes after leaving Harold's office. He explained the situation to the state police commander, and was pleasantly surprised to find that he was more than willing to help.

"Don't worry," explained Patterson, "we've done this kind of thing before. That's what we're here for. Shouldn't be any trouble at all to have a man cover your graveyard shift. You and I can work out the money bullshit when you get back."

Bill totally agreed with Matt about his decision to go to Montana and wished him well. Matt immediately called all three of his patrolmen, explained the situation and arrangements he had made with the State Police, and authorized Rick Dawley as acting chief.

Now, he was busy enumerating the details with his wife, Val, and it wasn't going nearly as well as he had hoped. In fact, Val was incredulous. The two stood in the kitchen, one on either side of the breakfast table, face-to-face like warriors ready for combat.

"Let me get this straight," Val inquired. "We haven't taken a vacation since we moved here, and now you're telling me that you and Chris are going to *Montana*? Are you out of your mind?!"

"But Val, it's *not* a vacation. We're going there to—"

"Look, we've been through an awful lot together . . and I've always been one hundred percent behind whatever you've wanted to do . . . but *this* is ridiculous! Do you even *know* these people?"

"Well . . . not exactly. I mean we *do* know Ralph Gilly He's the fellow whose fishing ranch we went to when we were in Montana ten years ago. He's the one who called Chris. This other fellow is his neighbor. But I've told you all of this already and—"

"Tell me again."

She was *really* being difficult.

"Can we sit down first?"

Val was silent.

"Well, can we?" he repeated, smiling *that* smile he always knew made her weak in the knees—and it seemed to be working.

But, as usual, he was wrong.

What he detected as the beginning of a smile on Val's face was just the sign of further resolution. She took a deep breath, closed her eyes, then opened them again—this time, even wider. Matt had never seen her so incensed.

"Val, please, let's just sit down and discuss this like adults." Too late, he remembered how much she always resented that phrase: like adults. "Sorry, honey, sorry. I didn't mean—"

"No, that's *exactly* what you meant!"

"Fine," Matt conceded. "You know what? You're right. You're behaving like a two-year old."

Val narrowed her eyes.

"Well, you *are*." Matt continued, "Look, we need to get this settled. The sooner we do, the sooner I can work out the details and get packed."

"Fine," said Val through tightly pursed lips. "Just fine." She pulled out the chair and sat down.

Matt could see she was weary from the brief battle. He also knew that would never have been the case prior to her bout with breast cancer. But things were different now, and they both knew it. Still, Val never stopped trying to assert herself—and Matt respected her for it.

"Look, honey," he said. "I know you're upset. And I don't blame you one bit. I really don't. But somebody's in big trouble out there, and they *really* need our help."

"But why *you*?"

"I told you, Val, the note said that if they called the police or the FBI, they'd kill the man's foreman. Hell, they've already killed his prize bull."

Val nodded meekly. Matt knew that she understood and that he had won. She just hated to see him go. She *always* hated for him to go. She stood up and came around to his side of the table. Matt took her in his arms and held her tightly.

"I'm sorry, honey," he whispered. "I'd never just take off like this unless it was absolutely necessary."

Val looked up and smiled. "I know," she admitted. She closed her eyes and offered him her lips. Matt kissed her softly in response.

"You're a good man," she whispered.

"Chris went on the Internet and found us a decent flight from Newburgh to Bozeman," said Matt. "Only two stops. I was kind of hoping you'd drive me down there in the morning."

"Well then I guess you better get busy packing."

Val's smile was back, and so, too, was her energy.

Good old Val, thought Matt. He'd won the lottery when he married her — and he knew it.

Chapter 7

Montana

Ralph sat in his study and listened in disbelief as his friend, Clint, rattled off detail after detail about his predicament. Ralph was incredulous. After all, this was Montana in the twenty first century, he thought. These kinds of things just didn't happen here. He needed to understand exactly what his neighbor was up against.

"Slow down, Clint. It's too much for me to absorb all at once. Now start from the very beginning and don't leave *anything* out."

Clint's face was ashen. Ralph hadn't seen him this distressed since Harriet died.

"I'm sorry, Ralph. I'm just beside myself." Clint took a deep breath and began. "Let me see, I guess it began when I didn't smell the coffee this morning. Shorty *always* makes the coffee before he does anything else—it was seven o'clock already and I couldn't smell a damned thing."

Ralph listened intently, running his fingers through his thick white hair. He was 73 years old, and tough as they came. He, too, was a bachelor—but by choice.

"I went downstairs," continued Clint, "half expecting him to give me some bullshit excuse for not having the coffee ready, but he wasn't even there. I checked his cottage. No Shorty. That's when I walked out to the barn and saw that Tyrus wasn't in his pen. It was no big deal. He's usually been fed and put out by seven, but I figured Shorty was probably inside the barn feeding him."

"Then what happened?"

"Well, first thing I noticed as I got closer to the barn was that the door was ajar. Now *that's* something I never expected to see. The padlock was unlocked and the door was open a good six inches. I called Shorty's name, but he didn't answer—and that's when I found Tyrus." Clint dabbed at the corner of his eye with a handkerchief. "His throat had been slashed and they'd . . . well . . . they'd gone and cut his pecker off and wrapped it in newspaper—with a note attached to it. Can you imagine that?"

Ralph gasped at the graphic image. "And what did the note say?"

Clint reached into his back pocket and extracted a crumpled piece of paper, thrusting it at Ralph. "Here, read it yourself." The note read:

"We killed your bull and we got Shorty. We killed the bull to show we mean buziness. Were tired of you White Men taking advantage of us. We want to hunt and fish like we always have. This is our land. We want fourty thousand dollers too and than you can have Shorty back. If we don't get the money well do the same thing we done with your bull to your man. Don't get no FBI or police or else. Well contact you soon and tell you where to bring the money. Remember no funny buziness."

The note was unsigned.

Ralph chuckled. "Not much for grammar or spelling," he observed.

"I guess," Clint replied. "But what do you make of it?"

Ralph shook his head. "You got, what, ten thousand acres?

"More like closer to fourteen."

"Plenty of neighbors, too," added Ralph. "Hell, it could be *anybody*. But whoever it is, it sounds like they're not fooling around."

Clint frowned. "So what do I do?"

"Depends," admitted Ralph. "Depends what they say when they contact you again. My guess is they're gonna try to bleed you for more and more money."

Clint shrugged his shoulders. "I know everybody thinks that just because I've got this big ranch I've got money coming out the wazoo. But hell, I'm mortgaged to the hilt. I'd be lucky to scrape together *twenty* thousand, let alone *forty*."

Both men were silent for a moment.

"Hey!" said Ralph. "How 'bout a cup of coffee? I got some fresh-brewed in the pot. Made it myself this morning. Get the old corpuscles going. Whatta ya say?"

Clint smiled.

"Atta boy. Black, no sugar, right?"

"Right," sighed Clint.

"Hell, we'll figure this thing out. I promise."

Clint had his doubts.

Chapter 8

Shorty awoke with a start. It was pitch black. His eyes were open, but he couldn't see — and his head hurt something awful. Instinctively he went to rub it with his right hand, but he couldn't, because both his hands were fastened tightly behind his back. His legs, too, were bound together. "What the fuck?" he tried to say, but even *that* was impossible. His mouth had been taped shut, and there was a blindfold across his eyes. Where was he? Why was he there?

Slowly, the event's of the previous night came flooding back into his consciousness. He vaguely remembered men coming into his bedroom in the dark. Muffled commands and whispers. He wasn't sure how many men there were: three, maybe four. He couldn't be sure. He recalled a strong chemical smell (probably chloroform) when a handkerchief or rag was forced over his face, as strong hands slipped telephone zip ties over his wrists and ankles, pulling them painfully tight. The rest was a blur, as he had quickly lost consciousness.

Now, a wave of nausea swept over him, and he gagged reflexively, trying desperately not to vomit. He was afraid he would suffocate. Suddenly, a light was turned on in the room, and a voice fuzzy with sleep called out, "What's wrong? Are you going to be sick? Hang on, damn it, I'll be right there."

A moment later he felt strong hands tearing off the tape that covered his mouth. He breathed deeply and the feeling of nausea abated. "Where am I?" It came out as a weak, raspy whisper. He hardly recognized the sound of his own voice.

"Never mind," came the reply. The voice was not familiar to him.

Chapter 9

Henry Smith, at age 22, was the youngest of four Native American men who had decided they'd had enough of the white man's invasion of their land. He preferred to be called by his adopted name, Golden Eagle, rather than his actual surname, which he viewed with disdain. Smith also happened to be the number one surname for Native Americans living in Montana, and a shameful reflection of his people's past and their conqueror, the white man. Henry wanted no part of their ways, with their material excesses and avaricious need to own everything. In every way, he was a Flathead, through and through. All he desired was to be left alone to hunt and fish like his ancestors had done for centuries.

So, when 55-year-old Walter Begay, a former resident of the Blackfeet Reservation in Northwestern Montana, initially proposed his plan to the three younger men, it was Henry who volunteered first to assist in the kidnapping. The older man had often expressed his frustration at being unable to access the land and waters controlled for centuries by his ancestors. He longed to hunt and fish, unrestrained by the artificial borders imposed by the white man. If he couldn't do that, then he would exact a bit of revenge by taking some of the white man's money.

Granted, Begay would admit, he got along fine with his employer, Bill Jessup, who owned Jessup's Feed & Grain, located on Route 41, northeast of Dillon, the home of The University of Montana Western. But Jessup was an exception in Walter's book. For the most part, he despised virtually every other white man he'd ever encountered, especially those from the federal government who had overseen the reservation where he formerly resided.

The other two men present around the table were Ronald White Feather, 25, also a Flathead, and Jim Blackwater, 27, a Crow. They both worked maintenance on the midnight-to-eight, graveyard shift at an auto parts distribution warehouse in nearby Twin Bridges.

Dillon, being a college town, was the main attraction for those who lived in the rural areas of Beaverhead County, and especially for those young Native American men who did *not* live on a government-controlled reservation. Unlike those unfortunate souls, Walter, Henry, Jim, and Ronald weren't constrained by the no-alcohol rules that governed the others. The four lived on a forty-acre parcel of land, located just a few miles up the road, that was owned by Walter and Henry's employer.

Walter resided in an ancient, Franklin mobile home that he had bought and had towed to the property. The three younger men occupied a rundown, doublewide that sat in front of the mobile home on the same parcel. They all paid rent to Jessup.

The memory of the evening that led to the kidnapping was still fresh in Henry's mind. They were sitting in the small area of Walter's trailer that served as the kitchen.

dining room, and spare bedroom. The small drop-leaf table was barely large enough to accommodate the four of them, as they sat hunkered over its scarred Formica surface, which was littered with empty beer cans.

Walter was reserved but forceful as he laid out his proposal. "I'm not suggesting that we kill anybody," he explained. He held an icy stein of Coors beer in his hand, the reddish brown color of his skin contrasting starkly against the golden color of the malt beverage. "Sure, we'll have to kill the bull—just to let them know we mean business—but under no circumstances does anybody get hurt."

Henry smiled in silence, his head filled with the images that the newly hatched plan evoked. He could just imagine the astonished look on the face of the rancher when he found his prized possession lying dead in the dust of the stall, as worthless as a pile of Confederate currency. Walter continued to drone on, sketching out the rough details of the when and how of the kidnapping plot. Let him make *all* the plans, thought Henry. He didn't mind. He would do whatever was necessary to protect himself.

To emphasize where he stood, he said, "I don't want any of the money, okay. I just want to see that old white man get what's coming to him. You can have my share."

*   *   *   *   *

When Shorty had first been awakened, he thought he was still in the throes of a dream. The muffled noises, whispered commands, and rapid movements of the four men moving about him had seemed choreographed, much like a dance sequence in a musical. But he had quickly recognized the nightmare for what it was.

Now, fully awake, the reality of the situation was becoming more apparent. He retched once or twice, but managed not to vomit. "Where am I?" he repeated.

"I told you never mind!"

"What do you want?"

"What difference does it make?"

Great! A question to answer a question.

"Is it *money?* I can *get* money—if that's what you want Just tell me how much. My boss'll pay plenty."

At least, I hope he will.

"Who said anything about money? Now shut up. before I tape your mouth shut again."

Shorty thought he detected an accent of some kind. Mexican—no, Native American, that's what it was. But, he thought, why in the world had they kidnapped *him?*

"Look, I don't know what you want, but can't we talk this out? Did somebody insult your ancestors, or refuse to serve you in a bar? Is that what this is about? How much money will it take to make it right, huh?"

"Typical white man," said Henry. "You piss all over us, and then think you can buy your way out of everything. If I wanted your money, I'd just take it—"

"Well, what the hell *do* you want?"

"I want you to shut the hell up—*now!*" And with that, Henry grabbed a nearby roll of duct tape and covered the ranch hand's mouth once more. "Now, be quiet!"

Chapter 10

Matt hated flying. For as long as he could remember, the thought of being suspended five miles in the air in an oversized tin can with wings made his knees go weak. It didn't help matters that the particular tin can in which he and Chris were flying wasn't much bigger than those in which sardines were packaged.

In order to get the cheapest airfare available, Freitag had booked them on a round-trip flight with Delta Airlines consisting of three legs each way. Thankfully for Chris, the first leg, from Newburgh, New York, to Detroit—the one they were on now—was only an hour and forty minutes long. The plane was a twin-engine CRJ-200, a 50-seat Bombardier jet operated by Endeavor Air. Chris despised the small jet, primarily because of the thirty-one inch pitch, or space, between the seats, which were less than eighteen inches in width. Even with the extra three inch pitch provided in Economy Plus class, he still had difficulty finding a comfortable position for his six foot, six inch frame. He jokingly referred to the plane as the "flying straw."

Once in Detroit, there'd be a forty-minute layover, which was just enough time to switch to a Boeing 757-300 for the two-hour flight to Minneapolis/St. Paul. After a slightly longer layover, they'd catch a Boeing 737-800 for the final flight into Bozeman Yellowstone International Airport. Both Boeing aircraft had more than enough legroom to suit Chris.

Chris and Matt both had federal firearms licenses and concealed carry permits, but, as a matter of law were required to check their guns before boarding. Once in Montana, they'd retrieve their weapons at the airport. Chris had a Smith and Wesson Bodyguard .38 revolver. Matt's choice was a Glock 42, also a .38 caliber, but a semi-automatic. Neither man intended to use his gun unless absolutely necessary, but knowing they weren't going out there unarmed provided at least some piece of mind.

The heavy droning of the two jet engines made conversation all but impossible between the two men, but it didn't stop them from trying.

"How long do you think we'll be there?" inquired Matt.

Chris turned to face his former partner and smiled. "Ten days, I guess."

It was Matt's turn to smile. "Okay, I guess that *was* a pretty stupid question," he admitted.

"Well," laughed Chris, "one thing's for sure, it definitely can't take any *longer* than ten days."

Both men were aware of the constraints imposed upon them by the term of their non-refundable, round-trip airline tickets, and the short leash placed upon Matt by his day job. Freitag had already taken retirement.

They sat in silence for the next twenty minutes.

"I wish we were going fishing," Matt whispered at last.

Eyes closed, Freitag seemingly responded by passing gas, then added a loud snort for emphasis, alerting Matt to the fact that his partner was asleep. In a matter of minutes, the two men were snoring quietly in concert. Before long, Matt began to dream.

    . . . It was early summer, 2001. The highway appeared endless. It had been Matt's idea to drive, and now he regretted it. South Dakota, with its endless Great Plains was as barren as any state in the Union, and seemingly went on forever. But when they reached Wyoming, things finally became interesting. Matt marveled at the lunar-like landscape, influenced by the enormous caldera in Yellowstone National Park. Then, suddenly, they were in Montana. The landscape changed from mountainous terrain to an almost desert-like atmosphere that was nothing like that of the Catskills. Yet some of the best trout waters in the country flowed through this unlikeliest of terrains.

As often happens in dreams, the scenes were a mixture of memories and imagination—and they changed as quickly as slides on a screen at a business presentation.

    . . . The water lapped at the top of Matt's bulky neoprene waders, and he struggled mightily to maintain his balance. The large brown trout he had induced to take a #20 Harrop PMD Biot Sparkle Dun was doing its best to seek shelter. It had already made a sizzling run that threatened to take Matt into his backing, and if it took enough line from the oversized arbor on the reel Matt was using, it might be able to reach the root structure of one of the many willow trees that lined the shores of the river.

The battle raged on, with Matt alternately gaining then losing line, but eventually the fish began to tire. Slowly but surely Matt began to regain line.

"I got him," offered Chris.

Just as Matt lifted the big brown's head free of the water, Chris swooped clumsily at the trout with his shallow, long-handled net – and knocked the fish free of the fly.

"Shit!" shouted Matt. Not only had his quest to join the elusive "twenty-twenty" club ended, but so had his dream . . .

"Shit!" he repeated, as he slowly opened his eyes. Then, realizing where he was, he quickly looked around the interior of the plane to see if anyone had heard his unintended expletive. Grateful that no one seemed to have noticed, he whispered, "Thank God."

"What'd you say?" mumbled Chris, before immediately lapsing back into his own euphoric state of mind.

"Oh, nothing," sighed Matt, "nothing at all. Just go back to sleep."

Chapter 11

Montana

Ralph Gilly was a nervous wreck. On one hand, he was anxious to see the two New York City cops whose company he had so enjoyed those many years ago. But he was also filled with trepidation at the thought of what their "visit" could bring with it. He had already doctored his reservations book to reflect the fact that the two men had booked their trip to Big Sky Fin and Fur Resort nearly a year ago. Their visit had to appear completely unrelated to his neighbor Clint's current difficulties.

The thing he remembered most about the men was the disparity in their heights. He always thought of them as Mutt and Jeff, the old cartoon characters he had watched between double features at the ancient movie house in his hometown of Twin Bridges. The theatre was long gone, but the memories lingered on—in particular, Episode 49, called *Texas Tom*.

As Ralph drove his white, 2005 Ford F-250 pickup along the winding dirt road that led from his ranch to the highway, which would eventually take him north to I-90, then east to the airport over in Bozeman, he rehearsed how he would greet his guests. He didn't suspect that he was being watched, but in the unlikely event that he was, he needed to appear as natural as possible when he met the two men — ostensibly for the very first time.

When he awoke that morning, the sun was well above the horizon, and the crisp shadows falling from the trees and shrubbery indicated that the day would be clear and dry. Now, as he neared the Interstate, the sun was on its way back down, and nearly gone. The Weather Channel had shown that there was no rain in the forecast for at least the next five days. Good, he thought, the last thing they needed was any kind of *weather*. The better the conditions, the easier it would be to camouflage the activities of his guests from the Northeast. They could fish some, and hopefully do their detective work without raising any suspicion.

Chapter 12

Treadwell, NY (Just outside Roscoe)

Although Al Coif was now 45 years old, he had been fascinated by fire ever since he was a small boy. Now, as an adult, the attraction he felt for it was all consuming, much like the flames themselves.

It had begun innocently enough at a very early age. Like many who lived in rural areas, Al's father, Charlie, burned his trash in small, controlled fires on his property, rather than be bothered bagging it and hauling it to the nearest landfill, which was half an hour away. He and Al would rake the refuse into small piles along the dirt and gravel driveway that led from the milking barn down to the rural road that bordered their small dairy farm on its southern flank.

Al helped his father separate the glass and plastic containers from the paper and cardboard, placing the empty containers in large, plastic bags that would eventually be hauled to the recycling center in Grahamsville. Once that had been taken care of, Charlie squirted lighter fluid on each of the small piles of rubbish, and allowed his son to ignite them with a flick of the scarred, Zippo cigarette lighter he carried with him at all times. It was a memento of Charlie's service in Vietnam, and bore a crudely scratched inscription that read: *"Nam, 1969-70, Why me?"* It served as a kind of totem that calmed him in times of stress, when Charlie would roll it around inside the palm of his right hand.

As was the case with many children who lived on farms, it was almost impossible for Al to form any kind of real friendship with his classmates, since literally miles separated him from the nearest kid his age. His being an only child just served to further cement the relationship with his father, and they became virtually inseparable. Each day, after school, the two worked alongside one another doing the various tasks required to maintain a farm. Lighting small trash fires and watching them burn became a ritual the two shared, which served the same purpose that smoking, or having a drink together in a bar, might serve for adults at the end of the work day.

Laura Duncan Coif, Charlie's wife and the mother of his boy, was a local gal with whom he had formed a relationship at age ten, while riding the school bus in rural Delaware County. Once they were married in June of 1969, neither ever looked at a member of the opposite sex again.

After a small wedding in Treadwell, the couple spent their solitary honeymoon night at a small hotel in nearby Delhi. The following morning, Laura returned home to settle in with her parents, Jim and Bette Duncan, while Charlie hitched a ride from a neighbor to the bus stop in Monticello.

Two days later, he reported to Parris Island, South Carolina, for basic training, where he remained for sixteen weeks, before shipping out to Vietnam.

Eight months and twenty-two days later, Al was born, prompting some casual speculation among friends and relatives on both sides of the marital aisle. He wouldn't be introduced to his father until he was well over a year old.

Living with her parents on their small dairy farm provided Laura with the opportunity to really bond with her newborn son, and also helped to counterbalance the loneliness imposed by his father's absence. If life wasn't ideal for the young mother, at least it was tolerable—and that was a blessing.

When Charlie returned from Vietnam, jobs were scarce, and it just seemed like the right thing to do to join Laura at her parents' farm, helping the aging couple to tend to their dozen or so dairy cows, and farming the various crops that helped them all subsist. It wasn't an idyllic situation, but it would suffice. Until it all came crashing down.

It was November, 1981, during deer season. Delaware County contained a disproportionately large population of deer—especially large bucks—and it wasn't unusual for Jim Duncan to grant access to his forty-seven-acre farmland to local hunters in return for a generous share of venison. But, on that day, things took an unfortunate turn. A shot fired from a Winchester Model 94, lever action .30-.30 rifle missed its intended target—a six-point buck—and ricocheted off a rock, striking Charlie Coif in the one place guaranteed to kill him instantly: his left temple. He never felt a thing. He was 31 years old. Al was 10, and his mother, now a widow, was 29. Ironically, Charlie had survived nearly two full years of combat in Vietnam, only to be struck down in the prime of his life by a bullet fired by a 14-year-old boy.

The death was ruled an accident, and no charges were ever filed. Several days later, at the funeral home, it seemed only natural that just before Charlie Coif's burial, Al would remove his father's old Zippo from its place in the casket, and secret it away in his pocket, where it would remain with him as a kind of touchstone from that day forward.

The fire setting didn't begin in earnest until puberty, when the absence of a father became even more of an impediment to Al's psychological development than it already was.

And it happened *almost* by mistake.

It had been nearly a year since his father's untimely death, and Al missed his father badly. The memories formed during their ten years together were a constant reminder to the young boy of his loss. As he raked the autumn leaves that had accumulated on his grandfather's driveway, he stopped periodically to roll his dad's Zippo lighter between his fingers, opening and closing the metal top of his prized possession with a crisp, metallic *snap!* He could feel the tension growing within him.

Now, with the top open, Al flicked his thumb over the textured wheel and watched as the spark it created ignited the lighter fluid into a bluish yellow flame. Before he could react, the Zippo slipped from his grasp and fell upon a pile of leaves at his feet. The dry tinder caught fire and immediately began to burn, sending up a lazy column of smoke into the dry, fall air. The aroma of the smoking leaves filled the boy's nostrils, and he closed his eyes and envisioned his dad beside him. The pent up tension he had been feeling slowly dissipated, and he could feel himself relaxing.

Al looked down at the burning leaves and, for a brief moment, thought about stomping out the flames. Instead, however, he used his rake to bring more fuel into the fire, until, before long, the entire driveway full of leaves was ablaze. He didn't feel any real sense of urgency; in fact, what he experienced was more akin to elation. A blanket of serenity had enveloped the young boy and he stood calmly watching the orange and red glow of the fire, feeling the tension he had felt before completely leave him. But he was smart enough to know that he ought to call someone for help.

"Mommy! Mommy!" he screamed. "Help! Help!"

Laura Coif flung open the screen door of the kitchen and burst through the doorway and down the few stairs to the driveway. In an instant, she had uncoiled the nearby water hose attached to a spigot on the foundation of the house and began spraying the burgeoning flames.

After about five minutes, the fire had been quelled, and she and Al breathed a collective sigh of relief. The two stood side by side: the mother with her arm around her son, the boy leaning against his mother's hip.

"What happened, Al?"

"It was an accident," admitted the boy. "I was playing with Daddy's lighter and it slipped out of my hand. Honest."

"Oh, honey, I believe you. You must have been so frightened. I'm just glad we caught it before it really got out of hand. You've really got to be more careful."

Al stared down at the ground.

"I should never have let you have that lighter," his mother admonished him. Then, she softened her tone, "But I did . . . because . . . I knew how much it meant to you."

Al lowered his eyes and sheepishly whispered, "I'm sorry, Mommy. I'll be more careful."

You promise?"

"Yes, Mommy, I promise."

But it was an empty promise that would be repeated far more times than Laura Coif ever could imagine.

Chapter 13

Montana

Ralph Gilly pulled his pickup into the airport's short-term parking lot at precisely 10:00 p.m., in plenty of time to meet Delta flight DL 2037, scheduled to land at 11:26 p.m. at Gate 5. He checked the arrivals board on the first floor of the terminal and saw that the flight was on time.

Good, I can catch a good nap before they arrive.

The long, turn-around trips to pick up guests were beginning to take their toll on the aging rancher, and he *needed* the rest more than he wanted it.

Ralph made his way toward the "Meet and Greet" area facing the Y-shaped corridor that funneled arriving passengers from their gates into the main body of the terminal. As he walked, he marveled at just how large "the whole danged affair" had become. A second story was added in 1983, doubling the facility's capacity, and a new control tower was constructed in 1997. Another modernization and expansion took place in 2011, and at present, the airport handled more than 350,000 passengers per year, and had been designated a "small hub" by the FAA.

The waiting area was nearly deserted by the time Ralph sat down on a softly padded seat. He set his iPhone's alarm for 11:20 p.m., leaned back, slid his weathered Stetson down over his eyes, and promptly fell into a dreamless asleep.

Sixty-five minutes later, the soothing, digital sound of the "Waves" alarm tone from Ralph's iPhone gently roused him from his slumber without startling him. The iPhone was a small concession to the advancing tide of progress that Gilly resisted with all his might. However, lately he had to admit that the little device was worth its weight in gold. He tapped the button at the top right hand corner to quiet the alarm, then pressed it again firmly and held it until the swipe bar appeared on the face of the phone, permitting him to shut it down completely.

One by one, passengers dribbled through the exit ramp, many laden with tubes containing four- and five-piece fly rods. Most were men. There was only one reason folks came to this part of Montana at this time of year, and that was to fly fish its miles and miles of blue-ribbon trout streams. Oh sure, there were *some* women, and some travelers were there on business. But most came for the fishing—except for "Mutt and Jeff."

As if on cue, the two lawmen from "back East" came walking more or less in Ralph's direction, their eyes scanning the interior of the terminal for a recognizable face. Chris had on a blue and orange Mets baseball cap, and Matt was wearing a generic, tan fishing cap with an oversized bill. The two hats were separated by ten inches—vertically. Ralph stood up, chuckling at the Mutt and Jeff analogy rattling around in his head, and started toward the two men, who apparently didn't recognize him.

"Chris, Matt," he greeted them. "Welcome to Montana. I guess it's been a while."

Ralph offered his hand in friendship, shaking each of the other men's hands firmly in turn. "I believe I had more color in my hair the last time I saw you fellas." He removed the Stetson, revealing a thick head of white hair. "Maybe that's why you didn't recognize me right off."

"Maybe," admitted Matt, "but back then, *one* of us had a lot more hair (he nodded in Chris's direction), so I guess we're kind of even. " Right, partner?" He reached up and lifted the Mets cap from off Chris's head.

"Yeah . . . *what*ever," Chris said with a grin. "I guess we can't *all* be blessed with a mop."

The three men stood quietly for a moment, before Ralph broke the silence. "Well . . . uh . . . I guess you fellas must be plumb wore out. What say we go get your bags and hit the road. We can talk a bit on the way back to the ranch."

"Sounds like a plan," said Chris.

"Or maybe we can just sleep," sighed Matt.

"We'll figure it out," Ralph laughed.

The three men started for the luggage carousel, along with the majority of the deplaning passengers, and as they walked, Ralph thanked Matt and Chris for coming. Both assured him that they would never have considered *not* coming, and promised they would do whatever it took to help his friend.

"Tell you what," said Ralph, "why don't I go get the truck and I'll meet you outside."

Before long, Chris and Matt found their luggage, claimed their firearms, and exited the terminal. They loaded everything into the bed of the waiting pickup, and, in a few minutes, the three men were on their way back to the resort. Within seconds, both Chris and Matt were fast asleep.

Ralph fastened his seat belt, then turned on the Sirius XM radio mounted on the dash of the pickup, and selected the FOX News Channel from among the half dozen presets. As he adjusted the volume, he smiled at the irony. Years ago, he'd have been lucky to find one AM station to listen to. Now, here he was with dozens and dozens of channels, not one of which *ever* lost its signal. *That's progress*, he thought. Or was it just another minor concession? He chuckled quietly to himself and drove on through the darkness.

Chapter 14

Shorty had been brought to the unused, third bedroom of the doublewide, where he would remain during his captivity. Walter had taken the precaution of replacing the hollow, Luan plywood door with a solid oak one, and installed a commercial grade deadbolt that was anchored into the double, two-by-four studs of the doorjamb.

Since there was no window in the room, the door represented the only egress. It would be relatively easy to guard the prisoner—especially since whoever was on duty at the time would be armed with the .22 caliber, Henry Repeating Arms rifle that Walter owned for the purpose of varmint hunting.

The four men had agreed to guard the prisoner on a rotating basis, with each assigned a six-hour shift. Since Ronald and Jimmy worked at night, and Walter and Henry worked days, the four men's work schedules dovetailed perfectly.

Shorty was using use all his self control to keep from panicking. He hated not being able to see, but could abide that as merely an inconvenience. Having duct tape across his mouth, however, was altogether another matter. It forced him to have to breathe through his nose—and that was no easy task. The deviated septum he had suffered as a result of a punch taken during a teenage scrap—over some girl whose name he had long since forgotten—made it almost impossible to take a full breath. *Breathe slow*, he admonished himself. *Nice and easy.* If they'd wanted him dead, he reasoned, they'd have already killed him. Although it was only a small comfort, it *did* help calm him a bit.

But why was he there? Slowly, his head began to clear and the memories of that early morning came flooding back. He recalled whispered voices and scuffling as he had been pulled from his bed. There were three—no, four— men, and each had on a ski mask. He recalled the lamp beside his bed being knocked off the night table, and the sound of breaking glass. *Clint's not gonna like that*, he had thought. And then a cloth over his face and that awful smell and the buzzing and then the blackness.

Now, he struggled to talk, but of course the tape made that impossible. All he could do was make as much noise as possible and hope that his captor would grow tired of the racket and take the tape off his mouth. He kept up the mumbled, unintelligible discourse, and after five full minutes that felt more like an hour, he was rewarded for his efforts—sort of. *R-i-p-p-p-p!* The duct tape was yanked roughly from his mouth, nearly taking his upper lip with it. "Owwww!" he screamed. "Fer Chrissakes, did you have to pull so damn hard?" Almost immediately, he realized what his outburst might cause to happen and added, "Okay, okay. It's fine. Really. It is. Just leave the tape off, okay? Please? I can't hardly breathe out of my nose, 'cause it was broke once. Please leave it off. I promise I won't say no more. Honest."

"You better not. Otherwise I'll—"

"Why am I here?"

"Okay. That does it. I'm putting the tape back on—"

"No! No! Please. I just want to know why I'm here. Did I do something to piss you off? I don't understand. Oh, I get it. Well, hell, I was probably drunk and—"

"Look," said the voice, "it's not about *you*. It's better if you don't know too much. Nobody's going to hurt you, so just relax. If everything goes the way it should, you should be back at your place in no time at all."

"Well, what do you think's going to happen? I mean, is somebody supposed to come and *get* me?"

"Just shut up, okay?"

"Oh, I get it. You're expectin' some kind of a ransom. Is that what it is?"

"Something like that."

"But there ain't nobody I know that's got any kind of money. Hell, I ain't even married."

"We don't care whether or not you're married."

We. The man had said *we.*

I was right, thought Shorty, *there's a bunch of 'em.*

"How many of you are there?"

"Never mind that. And it's not about *money.*"

"It's not?"

"No. Not for *me*, anyway. I don't give a crap about no money."

"Okay. I believe you. Hey, do you think I could get some water? I'm awful dry."

There was some rustling, and then Shorty felt the hard metal end of a canteen being shoved between his lips. He tilted his head back and swallowed greedily as the cool contents flowed into his welcoming mouth. Suddenly, the flow became more than he could handle, and he shook his head from side to side until the canteen was pulled away. "Sorry," he apologized, "I was starting to choke."

"Sorry. I didn't mean to hurt you."

"It's okay."

"You want some more?"

"Sure."

This time, the canteen's spout was offered up more gently, and Shorty sucked the cool water at a slower pace. Finally, he'd had enough and shook his head again to signal his captor. The canteen was withdrawn.

"I have to leave for a while," his captor informed Shorty. "Just stay nice and quiet, and I'll be back with some food."

"Okay. And thanks. Thanks a lot."

"Uh huh."

Then silence.

Shorty sensed he was alone.

He was right.

Chapter 15

Matt studied the so-called ransom note that Clint Davidson had given to Ralph Gilly with fascination. He read and re-read the words, but couldn't get a handle on their meaning.

"I don't get it. All they want is forty thousand dollars? That's chump change. I'm not really sure this *is* about money. It's almost like the money was an afterthought. My guess is there's something else they're after."

He handed the piece of paper to Chris, who likewise came to the same conclusion. "Beats me," he conceded. "My guess is we'll find out more when we hear from them again — and it'll probably be soon. That's when we'll learn what they *really* want."

"I'm with you," conceded Matt. "If it was just about the money, they'd have asked for more and been done with it. No, no, this is about something different — some kind of . . . *agenda*."

"Then again," Chris offered, "it *could* be about money after all. Most of the time, it's all about the Benjamins."

Ralph Gilly shifted uncomfortably in his chair. He looked at the two men and shook his head. "I think it's right there on that damned piece of paper. Read it again, Matt."

Matt complied with the request and began to read the note aloud.

Halfway through, Ralph interrupted him, pointing at the note. "See? It's right there! It says we're tired of you white men taking advantage of us. It's *our* turn now." He was really excited. "You *white men*," he continued. "It's *our turn* now. We're tired of you *white men* taking advantage of *us*."

"I think you're right, Ralph," Matt agreed.

Chris chimed in, "It almost reminds me of those PETA types. You know, set the dolphins free, or Free Willy, or some shit like that."

"But why kill Tyrus?" Ralph asked. "PETA would *never* do a thing like that."

Chris corrected him. "I never *said* it was PETA."

"Fair enough," Ralph admitted. "But why don't they just ask for what they want and see what the answer is?"

"Maybe because they've tried that already," Matt suggested. "Maybe they've asked for whatever it is and been stonewalled."

"So you think it's somebody Clint knows?" Chris asked.

"Sure sounds like it," Matt concluded.

"Well, if it is, they've really gone and fucked things up now," Ralph said. "You don't kill someone's prize bull and kidnap his best ranch hand and expect that everybody'll just be friends. These boys are in some serious trouble."

Matt looked at Chris, then back at Ralph. "I think we need to talk to Clint. Find out what's been going on. Got any ideas, Ralph?"

Ralph pursed his lips, removed his Stetson, and scratched his head. Worry lines creased his forehead. "I'll have to figure out something. Let me sleep on it and we'll talk in the morning. I don't want to do anything that'll arouse suspicion. Lord knows what these fellers might do to Shorty—if they haven't done it already."

"Well, that suits me fine," Chris offered. "I can think a hell of a lot better after a night's sleep, and God knows I can use some sleep. I don't know how *anyone* can sleep on one of those flying straws. I sure as hell can't."

Matt laughed quietly. "How about it, Ralph, got a couple of beds we can abuse?"

Ralph left his chair and started up the stairs. "Follow me, boys. We'll get on top of this first thing in the morning. I called Clint early this morning and asked him if he could 'help me out' with a couple of *landlubbers*. Anybody knows Clint, knows he fills in for one of my guides every so often, so it shouldn't arouse any suspicions. He's going to meet us at the boat ramp over the Henneberry Bridge access, which is about thirty minutes from Dillon, so you'll need to be ready pretty early."

"How early is early?" inquired Chris.

"Oh, 'bout four-thirty I'd imagine," Ralph informed him.

"Four-thirty!" chorused Matt and Chris.

"Relax. I'm just funnin' ya. I'll have the coffee ready about six."

"That's a *little* more sensible . . . I guess," groused Chris, forcing a smile that said he wasn't *all* that much upset.

The next morning, after Matt and Chris had taken turns showering, they dressed and headed downstairs to meet Ralph, who was waiting at the bottom of the stairs with a fresh pot of coffee.

Matt shook his head.

"Oh, shit," Ralph exclaimed. "I plumb forgot. You drink — what was it? — oh, yeah, hot chocolate, right?"

"Right."

"Well, let me see if I can rustle some up for you. Otherwise, would tea be okay for today? I can get some cocoa later on, but —"

"Tea will be just fine," Matt conceded. "I'm not exactly a chocaholic, you know. I just don't care for coffee."

"Make mine black," Chris suggested. "The blacker the better."

During a breakfast of eggs, bacon, home fried potatoes, and toast, Ralph outlined the day.

"You'll put in at Henneberry Bridge and float on down to Barrett's Diversion. Probably about six or seven miles. It's a nice float, and even though you probably won't catch any toads, you should see lots of action in the twelve- to eighteen-inch range."

"What's a toad?" Chris inquired.

Ralph laughed. "Man, you sure *are* a city slicker, aren't you? A *toad* is a big trout, usually over twenty inches, but more often measured in pounds. A big toad'll weigh in at four pounds or better."

"Oh."

Joe Perrone Jr.

"Anyway, you shouldn't run into *too* many other fishermen, and you guys ought to be able to spend most of your time getting the scoop from Clint about all that's going on with Shorty."

"I just hope we can help," Matt stated. "Normally the FBI or state police would be handling something like this. They've got loads of resources. There's a good chance we might not be able to do a damned thing."

"Well, I trust one thing: if anyone *can* help it'd be you two fellows."

Twenty minutes later, Ralph had dumped three duffel bags full of gear; a cooler-full of sandwiches and bottled water; and three, ten-foot, six-weight fly outfits into the bed of his pickup. He took a look at his wristwatch and announced, "It's nearly seven. We'd best get movin'."

Matt and Chris, dressed in breathable waders, long-sleeved shirts, and western hats, helped Ralph attach the trailer containing the Hyde Signature Series drift boat to the truck's hitch, and off they went.

When they arrived at the boat launch, Clint Davidson was already out of his pickup and waiting to lend a hand. Ralph made introductions all around, careful to say, "These are the two fellows I was telling you about. Came all the way out here from New York State to fish our Beaverhead."

Clint winked and reach out to shake hands with each man in turn. "Welcome to Montana. I think you're in for a nice time. Just wish the circumstances were a little different."

"Glad to be here," Matt said.

"Make that two of us," agreed Chris.

While the three men made small talk, Ralph backed the boat up to the ramp, unhooked it from the winch on the trailer, and handed the rope attached to the bow to Chris, who looked at it as though it were a live snake.

"Relax," explained Ralph. "When I back down into the water, the boat's gonna slide off the trailer, and you'll be left holding it with that there rope. So, hang onto it like your life depends on it."

Chris grimaced.

"It'll be okay. I promise. Just hold tight to the danged rope. I'm gonna back her into the water now."

Ralph got back into the truck, backed the trailer down into the water, and hit the brakes. Just as he had described it, the boat slid off the trailer and landed in the water. Chris held tight to the rope, smiling like the village idiot.

"Nice job," Matt complimented him.

Ralph had already pulled the truck away from the ramp, and, over his shoulder, advised Clint, "I'll meet you fellers downstream at Barrett's Diversion in about . . . oh, six hours or so, I reckon. Then we'll run you back up here to pick up your vehicle."

"Sounds like a plan."

"Oh, and leave a few for the rest of us, okay? And thanks for helping me out, Clint. I *really* appreciate it . . . if you know what I mean."

"Not a problem, Ralph. You'd do the same for me, buddy."

"You bet I would."

None of the men noticed a blue, weather-beaten pickup parked among a half dozen other trucks, off to the side of the launch area. It had followed them there from a distance, ever since they pulled out of the entrance to Ralph's ranch, and had coasted quietly into the parking area not long after they arrived by the river. They also failed to observe the middle-aged Native American who watched intently as their three-man party began drifting down the river a few minutes later and floated out of sight.

Once Ralph's pickup was gone, Walter Begay started the engine of his red Ford F-150 truck and drove out of the parking area, leaving nothing but a small cloud of dust behind. If Clint Davidson was up to something, Walter didn't have a clue what it was.

Chapter 16

Roscoe, NY

Acting police chief Rick Dawley scanned the headlines in the *Sullivan County Democrat*, the only such publication available these days to residents of Roscoe. Most of the news was irrelevant to the locals, but occasionally something would pop up that interested Rick. Up until recently, he had preferred to read the more provincial *Delaware County Times*, a weekly paper, but due to increasing pressure from the Internet, it had been forced to cease publication in July.

As he turned the pages, there were numerous stories concerning break-ins, petty larcenies, and even one about a lost dog (ultimately found living in a chicken coop), but one headline in particular caught his attention. It read: "Suspicious blaze destroys barn." Rick folded the paper in half and started reading the article:

> "Treadwell, NY—Police suspect arson in the fire
> Wednesday night that completely destroyed a barn on
> the property of William and Brenda Bostwick on Jackson
> Hill Road. Detective Harlan Wilson said that traces of an
> accelerant were found by Delhi police, ruling out an
> initial suspicion that faulty electrical wiring caused the
> blaze.

Police said a neighbor noticed an unfamiliar vehicle parked near the farmhouse, visible from the main road, several hours prior to the fire. He only recalled the vehicle as being blue.

Delhi Police urge anyone with knowledge pertaining to the incident to come forward. All contact information will be held in strictest confidence.

The Bostwicks' barn had stood on the property since 1915."

"Hey, Nancy," Rick called, "did you hear about the fire over in Treadwell?"

Nancy Cooper was Matt Davis's longtime secretary — *and* unofficial "boss" of Roscoe's police headquarters — shouted back her answer. "Nope! What about it?"

Rick got up from his desk and carried the newspaper into Nancy's office. He waved it in the air and informed her that, "It says here that somebody burned down the barn out at the old Wilson place over in Treadwell."

"Why on earth would anybody want to do a thing like that?" inquired Nancy. "The Wilsons have been there since . . . heck . . . since *Eisenhower*. Bill doesn't have an enemy in the world."

"Agreed. But unless I'm mistaken, that's the third barn that's burned down around here in the last two months. "The Richardsons lost their barn about three weeks ago. And Roger Soderman's burned down just two weeks before that. Never did figure out what caused *either* fire, as far as I know. You don't suppose we've got a serial arsonist on our hands, do you?" He answered his own question with a whispered, "I sure hope not."

*   *   *   *   *

Al Coif could feel the tension building inside him just as it had done on so many previous occasions. Losing the part-time job at the farmer's market over in Oneonta hadn't helped either. He was just beginning to feel comfortable about his finances, and had only three more payments to go on the flat screen TV he was buying from the Rent-to-Buy outlet before it would be his to keep. Now, however, there was a good chance that he'd not only lose the television set, but also forfeit the twenty-one months of payments he'd already made. If only his dad were alive, he thought. But, of course, that was just a fantasy.

The ancient Zippo lighter in Al's pocket was like a stick of dynamite just itching to be set off. He hated the feeling and the temptation it presented. He always tried to resist it, but never could quite make the grade. Now, the release it promised was just too much to ignore. He pulled the metal lighter from his pocket and began to open and close its cover nervously, but the tension wouldn't go away — not just yet.

Chapter 17

Montana

For the first mile or so of their float trip down the Beaverhead, there wasn't much talking. Matt and Chris took turns casting toward shore as Clint instructed them to do, but neither man had any success. Their flies drifted untouched over the numerous brown trout that hugged the banks, safe beneath the shadows of the overhanging branches of the willows and cottonwood trees that lined the river's shoreline.

Finally, Matt hooked a fish.

"Hallelujah!" shouted Chris. "Give him hell, partner!"

Matt's large arbor reel sang a metallic song as its drag was tested to its limit. The big fish was doing its best to strip first the thirty-plus yards of yellow fly line and then another seventy-five yards of braided backing from the screaming reel. All Matt could do was keep the rod tip high and hang on for dear life, while Clint expertly maneuvered the flat-bottomed drift boat in an effort to keep pace with the fleeing trout.

Slowly but surely, with Clint's help, Matt began to regain line and eventually the tired fish showed itself just beneath the surface of the off-color water.

"Atta baby, Matt," exhorted Chris, "You've got him now!"

Matt smiled and concentrated on the task at hand. The 4X fluorocarbon tippet connected to the Joe's Hopper fly was rated at six pounds, but who knew how much abrasion it had absorbed during the prolonged fight, which by now had lasted nearly five minutes. Raising the rod tip ever so slowly, Matt regained precious feet of fly line with each turn of the reel's handle as he lowered the rod to the water, only to raise it again to force the fish closer to the boat.

At last, Clint swept the long-handled, shallow-bellied, catch and release net into the water and under the tiring fish, scooping it up and into the boat all in one motion. "Now *that's* a Beaverhead brown," he exclaimed with pride. "None like 'em anywhere else in the world. Ain't she a beauty?"

Matt was too exhausted to respond, and Chris was fumbling in his rented vest for his camera.

"Pick 'er up and I'll get a picture of 'er for you," Clint suggested, as he removed the fly from the corner of the hen fish's mouth.

Matt lowered the rod onto the bench seat and reached out with two hands to accept the fish, whose gills were flaring rhythmically in an effort to breathe. He smiled and held it up in front of him. *Click! Click! Click!* went the shutter on Clint Davidson's camera, and the moment was preserved.

"Is *that* a toad?" Chris asked. "Looks pretty big to me."

Clint grinned. "Let's just say it's a good ole boy — I mean girl."

"Looks like a toad to me," Chris murmured.

Joe Perrone Jr.

After the fish had been carefully released back into the water, it was time to talk.

"So tell us what's going on, Clint. Ralph says you've got a missing foreman," Matt stated. "Want to tell us the latest?"

For a moment, there was nothing but silence. The two men studied Clint's face and could see he was in obvious emotional pain.

"I didn't mean to be so flip," apologized Matt. "I understand your foreman was also a good friend. This can't be easy for you."

A tear rolled down Clint's leathered cheek. He brushed it aside roughly. He appeared to be embarrassed to be showing so much emotion to total strangers.

"Next to my late wife, rest her soul, Shorty's become the best friend I've ever known. It's only been about two years now, but it seems like we've been friends all our lives."

Matt and Chris waited a respectable time before speaking. It was Chris who broke the silence first.

"Let's see if we can't help you get him back. Do you have any idea who might have done this?"

Clint shook his head.

"Ralph showed us the ransom note last night," Matt said, "and it mentioned about them wanting to fish and hunt your land. Is that something that you've had issues with?"

"Well, not really. I mean my land *is* posted, but everybody does that. I guess it kind of pisses off some folks, mostly because they can't just do what they want. I'd love to be able to open up the land, but it's not that simple. I have nearly fourteen thousand acres of land. If I opened it up to the public, it'd be a disaster. My livestock would be threatened, the trash, the noise—it'd be a mess. And then there's the federal government. I have certain arrangements concerning land use and so forth that would be totally jeopardized if I opened up my land and waters."

"Do you have *any* idea at all who might be behind this?" asked Matt. "Any enemies? Anybody you owe money to? Maybe somebody you pissed off in a bar?"

Clint laughed. "I don't even drink," he confessed. "Never have. Although now might not be a bad time to start."

"We've got to ask you these questions," Matt apologized, "just to get them out of the way. Sometimes the most obvious things are the hardest to recognize."

Clint drummed his fingers on the side of the boat. "We *did* run off a bunch of Indian fellers a while back. One of my ranch hands mentioned it to me. They were carrying fishing rods and a big bait bucket, headed out toward one of our little ponds. My guy chased them off."

"Did you see them yourself?" Matt inquired.

"No, but as far as I know there were four of them. One older guy and three others in their twenties."

"Hmmm. That would fit," Matt said.

"You mean about the Indian connection?" asked Clint.

"Yeah. Ask your man if he knows them. Could be they're the ones we want."

"Already did," replied Clint. "He said he'd never seen them before." Then he added, "Sorry 'bout that."

"No reason to be sorry," Matt assured him with a smile. "If it were *that* simple, you wouldn't even be talking to us."

Chris was absentmindedly casting at the shoreline as the boat continued its drift downstream. All of a sudden he jumped as though he'd been stung by a bee. The movement jostled Matt, and almost caused him to drop his rod.

"Jeez," he yelled, "what was that all about?"

"I think I got a fish!" shouted Chris. "Wait a minute. Yep. Fish on!"

"What'd he hit?" asked Clint.

"Damned if I know. Whatever it was you tied on."

The reel sang, and Chris alternately raised and lowered the rod, carefully regaining line each time, as Clint had instructed him to do at the start of the trip. All talk abated while Clint maneuvered the boat and Chris tried his best to corral the big brown trout that had impaled itself on his fly. The fight lasted all of two minutes.

Spraaaaang! The tippet connecting trout to fly fisherman snapped and Chris fell backward, nearly somersaulting out of the back of the boat.

"Shit!"

Matt was laughing aloud and Clint was looking down at the bottom of the boat, doing his best not to join the chorus.

Chris stared at the frayed end of the leader and then at Clint and Matt. He shrugged his shoulders. "Guess I had the drag too tight, huh?" he offered. "Oh well, my arm was getting kind of tired anyway. Pass me a bottle of water, will ya, Clint?"

"You're a good sport, Chris," sputtered Clint as he extracted a cold drink. He grabbed two more and exclaimed, "drinks all around."

"Very funny."

The rest of the day consisted of Matt and Chris alternately fishing and asking questions of Clint; and neither activity yielded much of anything—other than frustration. By the time Clint steered the boat to shore on the right side of the river at Barrett's Diversion, everyone knew they had a lot more work to do before they could take any measure of satisfaction from their efforts.

Ralph was waiting with the trailer, and within minutes, the boat was out of the water and loaded aboard it. Chris and Matt climbed into the back compartment of the big, four-door truck, while Ralph got into the driver's seat. "Hop aboard, Clint," instructed Ralph. "We'll run you back upriver to your vehicle."

Twenty-five minutes later they dropped Clint off at the parking area at the Henneberry Bridge access.

"I'll give you a call first thing in the morning," Ralph advised Clint, who had already fired up the engine of his truck.

"The earlier the better," replied Clint. "Time's a wastin'."

On the ride home, Ralph, Matt, and Chris bandied various possibilities back and forth. Was it a disgruntled neighbor who had left the note? Maybe members of a hunting and fishing club? By the time they got back to the ranch, all three men were too tired to continue the conversation. Day one had ended with nothing learned.

Chapter 18

The following morning, Matt and Chris met Ralph in the kitchen at seven sharp. The aroma of hot coffee was overpowering, and a fresh pot sat waiting on the heating element of the expensive coffeemaker sitting on the counter. The table held a freshly prepared mug of hot chocolate for Matt, along with an empty mug for Chris to use. Ralph was already on his second cup.

"There's whipped cream in the fridge," he advised Matt. "Don't use it too much—except for on strawberries—but it oughta be okay, I imagine. Probably only been in there 'bout a month." He winked at Matt, who smiled in appreciation.

"Hope you fellows don't mind instant oatmeal," offered Ralph. "I don't know if you remember, but I'm a bachelor. We've got a cook over at the lodge, but here at the house . . . well . . . you know . . . I'm about as useless as tits on a steer."

"Oatmeal's fine, thanks," Matt conceded. "The hot chocolate makes up for a lot."

"Yeah," Chris agreed. "I'm lucky if I get a cold bagel back home. We're just two ex cops, and neither one of us knows how to cook worth a damn."

Ralph shook his head in mock disapproval. "Whatever you two fellows got going on is certainly *no* business of mine." Wink.

"He's talking about his wife," Matt advised Ralph.

"Starting tomorrow," Ralph informed the two men, "I'll make sure we get you over to the lodge for breakfast. Actually, it might not be a bad idea if we moved you over there anyway. Make it look more like you're guests, rather than anybody special."

Matt and Chris nodded their agreement.

"In fact," continued Ralph, "why don't we do that right now. Grab your stuff, guys, and meet me back downstairs here in, say, twenty minutes?"

"Make it a half hour," Matt said. "I think that's a real good idea—moving us over to the lodge."

"Good," agreed Chris. "Then, we can get busy with what we came here for."

Breakfast lasted about ten minutes, and then, after moving the two men to the lodge, it was time to get down to business.

All three sat around a large, ranch-style table set up for the staff in the working kitchen of the lodge.

Matt spoke first.

"You know, Ralph, we're really kind of hamstrung here. Ordinarily, we'd have dusted Shorty's house and the barn for fingerprints. And we'd have taken some tire impressions from the dirt driveway. We'd have checked for prints as well. Then, if we'd found anything, we could have run it through the system, come up with some suspects. Then we could start asking around town and — "

"But we can't," interrupted Ralph. "Otherwise we could put Shorty's life in danger — if he's even still alive."

"Oh, he's alive alright," Matt assured him. "If he weren't, they wouldn't have any leverage at all. Shorty is *definitely* alive."

"I sure hope you're right."

"Okay, Matt began, "let's go over everything we know so far."

Ralph pulled out the ransom note and plopped it down on the table in front of the other two men.

"Seems pretty clear to me," he offered. "They want Clint to open up his property to hunting and fishing, otherwise they'll do the same to Shorty as they did to Tyrus — or worse."

Matt studied the note. "Let's *really* look at this thing," he suggested. "For instance, it says *'you people.'* Now what do you suppose they mean by that?"

"Well," Chris said, "I would think that it means they're somehow different from everybody else — especially Clint. So, let's look at it from the other side of the equation. Who's different around here from Clint?"

Ralph offered, "Since we're in Indian country, it's probably a safe bet that they're talking about 'Native Americans.' Yep, my money is on a bunch of Indians."

Matt was first to respond. "Yeah, I guess that's one possibility. But there's *another* possibility. I remember when I first moved to Roscoe, there was a lot of resistance from the locals to outsiders, people who weren't native to the area. I don't imagine folks here are any less provincial than New Yorkers—maybe even more so. After all, some of these people have probably been here since before the Civil War."

Ralph nodded in agreement. "I'm with you on that. I bought this ranch over thirty years ago, and it took me . . . oh . . . I'd say fifteen years, easy, before anybody so much as invited me in for a cup of coffee. It's different now, of course. I've made some really good friends. Trouble is, we all live so far away from one another, the only time I see most of 'em is at a Masons meeting or at church on Sunday."

"It seems to me," observed Matt, "that the crux of this thing is hunting and fishing. I guess that's as good a place to start as any."

Chris picked up the note and scanned its contents. "I guess we could pretend to be interested in moving into the area and start inquiring about fishing and hunting clubs."

"Good idea," Matt agreed. Let's get a rental car and start calling on some of the local fly shops—bars, too. And while we're at it, let's talk to a few realtors."

Ralph smiled. "God knows there's plenty of them— bars, I mean. Hell, fly shops, too—*and* realtors! I'll run you fellows over to Dillon. You can rent a car there."

The *car* turned out to be an SUV, which was "all anybody ever wants," according to the petite agent manning the rental office. Since it came with all the bells and whistles neither Matt nor Chris could ordinarily afford, she had no trouble convincing them to sign the rental agreement. "And don't forget, you can drop it off at the airport, if you need to!" she had shouted as they went out the door.

The first place Matt and Chris tried was a Coldwell Banker office on the south side of town that came up first on the results page of a Google search. Since both men were familiar with the brand name, it seemed a logical choice. The agency was located in a stand-alone building alongside a chili joint. The aroma emanating from the restaurant made it a hard choice which to visit first, but business came first so they parked in the side lot of the real estate office and walked inside. The door was ajar, and, upon initial inspection, the place appeared to be deserted.

"Hello? Anybody home?" Chris inquired.

"Hello," repeated Matt.

The office had four desks arranged in rows of two, each desk had one chair behind it, and another chair placed alongside. Typical real estate office. A rack of brochures representing various local businesses and attractions stood between the two rows. Matt gazed casually at the brochures, as he waited for someone to greet them.

There was a shallow vestibule at the rear of the office, containing three doors. The one on the left was marked "Ladies," the right one was designated for men, and the middle one, Matt thought, most likely led to a storage area or perhaps a conference room. He walked over to the center door and was just about to knock when it was opened suddenly by a young woman who appeared to be in her late forties, tall, with long dark hair, worn loose. She seemed genuinely startled to see Matt standing there.

When she saw Chris positioned behind him, her brown eyes grew wide with alarm.

"Oh!" she exclaimed, pulling back a bit. "I didn't know anyone was here."

"I'm sorry," Matt apologized. "I didn't mean to scare you. Really. I was just going to knock on the door to see if anyone was here when you opened it. We *did* say hello, but nobody answered."

"I guess that darned buzzer's not working again," said the woman, sounding somewhat relieved. Then, regaining her composure, she smiled and asked, "Were you here long?"

"Actually, no," Matt admitted. "Not more than a minute or two. I honestly didn't realize there was a buzzer, or I would have rung it first."

The woman walked past the two men, opened the front door, and reached around to try the buzzer. *Bzzzzzzzzz!* it sounded loudly. "Well, at least it's still working," she laughed.

Chris advised her, "It's probably a good idea to keep that door locked . . . uh . . . especially when you're alone."

"Good advice." The woman smiled and extended her hand. "I'm Charlotte Smathers. What can I do for you?"

"Well," Chris said, shaking the woman's hand. "We're thinking of getting a little piece of property here that we can put a trailer on to use as a getaway. Maybe do a little fishing." He winked. "You know, get away from the wives, once in a while, maybe hunt some, too."

"And your names are?" the woman said with a grin.

"Oh, I'm so sorry," stammered Chris. "Where are my manners? I'm Chris and this is Matt. We're staying over at the Big Sky Fin and Fur Resort with Ralph Gilly."

"Great place," acknowledged the woman. "Ralph runs a terrific business. Have you been there before, or is this your first visit?"

It was Matt's turn to respond. "Actually it's our second time. The last time we were here was probably ten years ago."

"Well, don't make it so long between visits," she chided them. "We can use all the business we can get."

The two men shrugged their shoulders and smiled.

"Actually, that's sort of why we stopped by," Matt said. "Since, at some point, we're going to have a place here, we were wondering if there are any fishing clubs in the area. You know, that we could join? There's an awful lot of water here, and it would sure be nice to know that we could meet some guys who could help us learn the area."

"Well, there are," Charlotte informed Matt. "But most of them are private. I can give you a list, but it'd be up to them whether or not they'd want to think about letting you join. We're a pretty close-knit group. But I'm sure you can understand that. After all, what else do we have here but great views, land, and water?"

"And lots of cattle," Chris offered.

"Well, there is that."

"It sounds an awful lot like where we come from," Matt said.

"And where exactly is that?"

"Oh," Matt said, "I guess we never said. We're from New York State. Up in the Catskills. We're pretty protective of *our* trout streams, too."

Charlotte laughed. "You're not serious? I'm originally from New York."

"No shit?" Chris blurted out, and then immediately added, "I'm sorry. I meant to say, *no kidding*?"

"Whereabouts in New York?" Matt asked.

"Oh, no place *you've* ever heard of," Charlotte admitted. "A little place along the southeast shore of Lake Ontario, called Mexico. But I've been *here* since I was ten."

"Mexico. By the Salmon River," Matt said. "I know it well. Well, not exactly *well*. But it feels like I do."

Charlotte questioned him with her eyes.

Matt quickly added, "Actually, the only reason I know about Mexico, New York is because a fellow we work with goes up there every fall to fish for steelhead. Otherwise, you would have been right."

Chris looked at his wristwatch. "I don't suppose you have that list handy, by any chance?"

"Sure. Just give me a minute."

Charlotte disappeared through the same door she'd come through earlier, and was back in a couple of minutes with two sheets of paper. She handed one to each of the men. "Tell them you know me," she laughed. "Maybe it'll help—"

"Or maybe not," laughed Chris, who quickly added, "Just kidding."

"Well, thank you for your time," said Matt. "Oh, do you have a card?"

"Sure," Charlotte said. She reached over onto one of the desks nearby and picked up a couple of cards from a holder, handing one to each of the men. "If I can help you find a piece of property — assuming, of course, that you can find a club that'll have you — give me a holler and I'll start putting together a list of some properties that you might like — if you can afford them. Land's not cheap here . . . but then I imagine you know *that* already."

"But worth every penny, right?" Chris joked.

"Yep. But some are worth more than others. That's why I have my job," laughed Charlotte, "to show you the difference."

"Much obliged, ma'am," said Chris, imitating a western accent as best he could.

"My pleasure, boys," replied Charlotte. "Now, if you'll excuse me, I have to be — "

"We're already on our way out," Chris said.

"Thanks again for your time," added Matt. "I'm sure we'll be seeing you again."

As soon as they were outside the office, Chris asked, "Why don't we try that chili joint next door?"

Matt smiled. "Somehow, I figured that was already a foregone conclusion. You buying?"

"Sure," replied Chris. "Why not."

"Good. Let's go."

Afterward, the two spent the remainder of the afternoon hopping in and out of various hunting and fishing shops, chatting with the owners and many of their customers as well. One man they met in a fly shop made no bones about his feelings about "outsiders."

"I wouldn't plan on being accepted in any of the clubs around here," he advised the men. "We call them *private* for a reason. Of course, you could hook up with some injuns. They're always sneaking onto our land and trying to fish our water. You just might get shot, though. They're a real pain in the ass, most of 'em. Never got over our 'westward expansion,' if you catch my drift."

Matt had wanted to rebut the man's logic, but thought better of it.

By the time it was dark, both he and Chris had had enough of the "local hospitality."

Chapter 19

Treadwell, NY

Al Coif drove slowly through the lush countryside that stretched for miles to the north and west of Roscoe. In the trunk of the blue '81 Datsun KB310 were three plastic containers of gasoline and a cardboard box filled with newspapers. The Zippo lighter rested in his right front pocket.

He tapped his foot impatiently on the thin, rusted out floorboard of the little hatchback coupe. In one spot, the salt, used in winter to make the roads passable, had completely eaten through to the interior of the car, and Al could see the asphalt beneath the vehicle as it sped over the road. All four tires wore rust-colored eyebrows in the person of rotted wheel wells. Similarly, both rocker panels were eaten away nearly to the frame. But the engine ran like a top, mostly due to Al's savant-like talents as a mechanic. Too bad there wasn't a garage that would hire him.

As he rounded a bend to the right and headed up a steady grade, he saw what he needed to see on the horizon. It was an old abandoned barn that sat about two-to-three-hundred feet back from the road. The farmhouse that it belonged to had long since burned to the ground, with only a brick chimney standing like a lone sentry guarding its former location.

Perfect.

Al pulled the little Datsun off the road and down the overgrown, rutted driveway that led back to the barn. He made a quick U-turn that left the car facing the road, and stopped. There wasn't a soul in sight. He set the handbrake, and climbed out, deliberately leaving the engine running, just in case.

He unloaded the gasoline-filled cans and carried them to the barn, placing them by the dilapidated doors that hung askew on their rusted hinges, looking for all the world like a mouth open sideways to a dentist. Humming now, he returned to the Datsun and extracted the cardboard box containing the newspapers and returned to the front of the barn. The structure listed slightly to the south, as if trying to avoid the prevailing wind that blew out of the north.

Careful to watch for any snakes or rodents that might be concealed in the grass inside the rotted edifice, Al began to prepare the barn to burn. He crumpled quantities of newspaper into long, twisted cylinders, then doused them with gasoline and placed them strategically around the inside perimeter of the barn. He then splashed the lower portions of the walls with the remaining gasoline.

Everything was ready.

Removing the Zippo from his pocket, Al quickly ignited one gasoline soaked bundle of newspaper after another, moving counter clockwise around the inside of the barn, beginning at the barn's left door. By the time he reached the other door, the entire interior of the barn was ablaze.

Al could feel the tension leave his body. He pictured his father in his mind's eye, with a smile on his face, saying, "Nice job, son. Real nice job."

Al smiled and closed his eyes. He stood motionless like that for about a minute, until the heat from the fire reached him and interrupted the reverie. When he opened his eyes, all he saw were yellow flames licking further and further up the dry walls of the barn.

Al turned and sprinted out the door, heading for the Datsun. He jumped into the driver's seat, released the handbrake, and drove straight down the driveway. As soon as he reached the road, he stopped, looked both ways, then slammed the door and made a hard left turn onto the macadam. There wasn't a car in sight, and he calmly started driving toward home.

About a tenth of a mile down the road, Al stopped the car on the gravel pull-off and looked back over his left shoulder to see the fire. All sense of urgency had left him, and for the first time in weeks, he felt at peace. He didn't notice the missing gasoline container until he got home and unloaded the Datsun.

Shit! he thought. *Ah, screw it. Can't go back now and get it. I'll just have to get me another one.*

About forty minutes later, a passerby saw the burning barn and notified the State Police, who notified the local fire department. News of the event didn't reach Roscoe for another day.

When it did, it didn't make Rick Dawley very happy.

Chapter 20

Roscoe, NY

Valerie Davis was not used to her husband, Matt, being away. Occasionally, he'd be out of town for a day or two, but never longer than that. And he always called her every night without fail. This time, however, he'd been gone three days already, and he still hadn't called home.

The two had recently celebrated Val's three years of being cancer free from the breast cancer that had reared its ugly head back then. Instead of the usual night out at Raimondo's Italian Restaurant in Roscoe, they had gone over to Parkville to try out a new place Val had found on Yelp, the online site that evaluated restaurants, hotels, and other consumer services.

The name of the place was the Dead End Café, and, when Val told him about it, right off the bat, Matt was reluctant to try it, if for no other reason than the nature of its name.

"What kind of a place calls itself the *Dead End Café*?" he had remarked. But if that was where Val wanted to go, he wasn't about to deny her the pleasure.

The restaurant turned out to be a pleasant surprise. Not only did the owner serenade the patrons with beautiful arias from well-known operas, he personally visited each table and spoke to his guests at length about the music itself. He had a rich baritone voice that reminded Val of the singers in the supper clubs that had been so popular back in the fifties.

The meal, too, was far better than either of them could have hoped for, topped off by generous slices of warm, homemade blueberry pie with gobs of fresh whipped cream.

Just thinking about that night now made Val miss Matt that much more. She lifted the handset off the wall phone in the kitchen and punched in the number for Matt's cell. Almost immediately, her call was directed to Matt's voice mail, leaving Val feeling empty and even more alone. She left a brief message asking him to call her when he got it, and ended it by telling him much she loved him.

God, I hate it when I can't reach you. Please be safe.

She went to bed filled with a sense of dread. As the wife of a career policeman, it was something she'd grown used to, but never quite accepted.

Maybe he'll call tomorrow, she thought, before eventually drifting off to sleep.

In Montana, at nearly the exact same moment, Matt sat on the edge of the bed and turned his cell phone on one last time, in a futile attempt to acquire a signal. The iPhone's screen displayed no bars where a signal should have appeared.

Shit! I hate when I can't reach her.

Tomorrow, he'd have to remember to ask if there was a landline he could use.

"Good night, sweetheart," he whispered aloud as he pulled the covers up around his neck and nestled his head comfortably into the accommodating pillow. "I'll talk to you tomorrow."

Chapter 21

Montana

It had now been nearly three days since Shorty was taken from the comfort of his bedroom and brought here, wherever "here" was. He'd tried to elicit as much information from his captors as he could, but all he had gleaned was the fact that he was not going anywhere until they heard from Clint. He had no idea where he was, or even what it was that his kidnappers expected to gain from their actions.

On the second day of his captivity, they had finally removed the tape permanently from his mouth with the promise to put it back if he started asking too many questions, or made any kind of a fuss. As best he could determine, there appeared to be at least three other men involved in his kidnapping, making a total of four. All of them spoke with the stilted speech pattern typical of the Native American population that inhabited the valley.

This morning, it had been "Injun One" who brought Shorty his breakfast. It consisted of cold cereal, dry toast, and a cup of god-awful coffee. Food preparation was definitely not a strong suit of this bunch, he had decided. He had assigned the names Injun One, Injun Two, Injun Three, and Injun Four, in turn, to each of the four men alternately charged with his care. Shorty called them by the pejorative names only in his mind, of course, never daring to verbalize the condescending monikers for fear of reprisal. But he was pretty sure they were a bunch of Indians.

Once the tape had been permanently removed from his mouth, the ranch foreman tried to ingratiate himself with each of the men guarding him, hoping that by doing so he could engender a sense of comradery that would make them less inclined to do him harm.

Early on, he concluded that three of the men were relatively young, based upon the nature of their conversation and choice of words, many of which were millennial buzz words like "trash," and "Netflix and chill." The only reason Shorty was familiar with the jargon was because, being a bachelor, he often frequented the same bars and poolrooms as did the younger generation.

"Injun Four," however, was older; Shorty guessed his age at between 45 and 60. His speech was slower, more measured and authoritative, and, not coincidentally, he also appeared to be in charge. In addition, he smoked incessantly, and had a hacking cough. The other three chewed tobacco, a conclusion Shorty had reached after days of hearing them spitting continually (into a cup, he hoped).

He had never done either, preferring instead to chew gum. Ever since they'd taken his favorite brand — Blackjack — off the market, he never went anywhere without a pack or two of Juicy Fruit. The current version was a poor substitute for the original, but it would do. He could still find Black Jack online at specialty stores (at outrageously high prices), but unless someone else bought it for him, they could keep it, as far as he was concerned.

"What's the chance of gettin' this blindfold off my eyes?" Shorty asked Injun One. "For sure, I'm not gonna remember what you look like. And, if you're worried about that, you could put on a ski mask or something — just to cover up your face."

Silence.

"Well, how about it?"

"Nice try, Whitey," said Henry Golden Eagle. Next, you'll be wantin' us to undo your hands — feet, too. I think we'll just leave things right the way they are."

For the first couple of days, Shorty had remained relatively calm, drifting in and out of sleep, content to spend the time lying on the bed. The chloroform they had used during his kidnapping had left him rather weak and somewhat hung over. But now, he was growing stronger and more alert. He needed something to occupy his mind. There was always someone present in the room with him, in case he needed to be taken to the bathroom, and to feed him his meals, but any real conversation was a waste of time.

"Am I still in Montana?" Shorty asked.

"Yes, you're still in Montana," Injun One informed him. "Where did you *think* you were?"

"Oh, I don't know. Maybe on the Riviera, or in Rome."

Both men laughed.

Lunchtime brought a changing of the guard. It was Injun Three this time. Judging by the high tenor of his voice, Shorty guessed him to be the youngest of the lot. He decided to press him hard about a few things.

"Hey, Pecker Head, how much money are you guys expecting my boss to shell out for my ass?"

"Who said anything about money?" Ronald White Feather responded.

"Oh, come on, everybody knows it's *always* about the Benjamins. What'd you ask for? A hundred thousand? A quarter of a million?"

"It's not *about* money."

"Well if it ain't about money, then what the hell *is* it about?"

Silence.

Shorty felt a chill run down his spine. *Maybe they're part of some goddamn cult. Gonna cut my nuts off.* He pictured the YouTube videos he'd heard about but had never seen, of prisoners dressed in orange jumpsuits waiting to be beheaded. *Oh, shit! Muslims.*

"You're not part of some kind of religious movement, are you? You're not *Muslims*, right? Please tell me your not no goddamn Muslims."

"Look, if you don't stop asking all these questions—"

"Yeah, yeah, I know. You'll put the tape back on my mouth."

"Look, man, we're *not* Muslims, okay? And we're definitely not terrorists. We're not a bunch of Jesus freaks. or anything *like* that. We just want—"

"What exactly *do* you want?" Shorty could almost sense that he was making some headway. If he knew what they wanted, he might have a better chance of talking his way out of the mess he was in.

He was wrong.

Ronald White Feather laughed.

"Pretty cute," he admitted. "You almost had me. I think you just better stop talking now, or I'm definitely gonna have to tape your mouth shut again."

"Okay, okay. I'll shut up. I promise. But listen, isn't there some way you can figure out that'll make it easier for me to *do* something? You know, maybe read a magazine — or watch some TV? How about it? I'm going nuts just lying here all day"

Silence.

Just as Shorty was about to give up, he got an answer.

"I could bring you a radio," came the soft reply.

"*Hallelujah!* Now you're talkin'."

"I got a little portable I could bring you. It'll probably only get one station though — KDBM, 1490 FM, Dillon's Real Country — that's all I get on my iPod's radio."

Kid's got a friggin' iPod, fer Chrissakes, thought Shorty.

"I'll settle for anything I can get," he conceded. "Hell, I'd even listen to opera. Well, maybe not *opera,* but *any* kind of radio would beat lyin' here in the dark. Could you really do that?"

"I can't promise. But I'll see what I can do."

"Thanks, partner. I'd be much obliged. And . . . uh . . . I'm sorry about calling you Pecker Head. What's your name, anyway? Not your whole name, just your first name."

"Just call me Ronald."

Then, imitating Robert Redford's character from the movie, *Jeremiah Johnson*, Shorty announced, "I will call you Ronald. It's a fine name and one that . . ."

Ronald White Feather must have seen the movie on some late night TV show, because he laughed at Shorty's improvised impression of the well known actor, and the two men grew just a bit closer because of it.

The following day, Ronald brought the radio. He also removed the nylon zip ties binding Shorty's hands behind his back, but not before he had replaced them with a pair of police surplus handcuffs. He positioned Shorty's wrists in front of his body, which allowed him to eat, read, and manipulate the controls on the portable radio. The handcuffs, however, were anchored to a leg of the bed's headboard by a length of chain.

He then replaced the zip ties on Shorty's ankles with another pair of handcuffs, thus making it impossible for him to do anything but shuffle. Running was not an option. Visits to the bathroom, when necessary, were always made at gunpoint, with the chain attached to the handcuffs serving as a kind of leash. Bowel movements were problematic, to say the least. Privacy was out of the question.

That same evening, well past midnight, Walter Begay parked his truck nearly half a mile from Clint's ranch, jogged to Clint's mailbox and quickly placed the envelope, containing the second ransom note, inside. Then, like the spirit of one of his ancestors, he loped silently back to his vehicle and was gone.

Chapter 22

Roscoe, NY

Rick Dawley sat at the far end of the counter in the Roscoe Diner, spinning left, then right, on the padded stool as he studied the menu, his feet just touching the floor. He'd only been acting chief for three days, but already he could understand that it wasn't a job he could take lightly.

Yesterday, he'd gotten a phone call from the State Police. He was told that another barn had been burned to the ground, and was asked to report any suspicious activity. This time, there hadn't been any doubt that it was arson, because whomever it was that had committed the crime had left an empty gasoline container in the dirt driveway that led up to the barn. The "Staties" had already run the prints that they were able to lift off the container, but no match had been found in any of the systems they'd checked.

Pretty damned stupid, he thought. *Unless it fell out of his truck.*

Apparently, the barn was part of a large tract of land that was actually listed for sale, and belonged to an investment group whose members lived down in New York City.

As Rick sat postulating about the crime, he whispered, "Thank God nobody was hurt."

"I'm sorry, did you say something?" inquired the waitress who was just passing by.

"No, no. I was just thinking out loud. Sorry."

"No problem. Are you ready to order yet?"

Rick studied the young girl's face. She looked familiar, maybe the daughter of someone he knew.

"Uh . . . yeah . . . sure," he replied. Rick set the menu down on the counter. "I don't even know why I bother to look at the menu anymore. I always end up having the same thing. Let me have the Turkey Wrap, please. And can you cut it in half and put the other half in a doggy bag?"

The young waitress smiled. "Sure. Not a problem."

"Oh, and use the *low fat* dressing, please," Rick explained, "Trying to watch the weight." He patted his belly for emphasis.

"Aw, you look just fine—but I'll box that other half up just like you asked." Another smile, this time a little broader.

Rick smiled back.

Then, the waitress leaned over and whispered, "Nobody calls it a doggy bag, anymore, hon."

"I *knew* that," Rick murmured, suddenly feeling a lot older than he had just thirty seconds ago.

Fifteen minutes later he had finished the half sandwich of turkey, lettuce, tomato, and mozzarella cheese. Even though it was low fat, he decided to leave off the Russian dressing that came in a little plastic cup. He paid the bill, walked out the front door, and got into his silver 2005 Ford

Bronco. He started the engine and pulled out of the lot, heading west out of town and toward Treadwell, the scene of the most recent fire.

It only took about fifteen minutes to reach the property. Yellow crime scene tape was stretched around the perimeter of what was now just a stone and masonry foundation supporting the remnants of some burnt timbers. The rest of the barn had collapsed into the middle in a pile, or mound, that still had traces of smoke coming off it.

Rick exited the Bronco and walked slowly up the gentle slope leading to the barn, being careful to avoid stepping on any tire marks. Although there were quite a few sets of tracks, most were quite large, and probably belonged to the various fire trucks that had responded to the call. However, off to one side, Rick noticed an altogether different set of tracks. These were also recently made, but measured only half the size of the others.

Rick walked back to his car to retrieve his cell phone and an impression kit for preserving the tire track evidence. When he returned to the area in front of the barn, he took a half dozen or so photographs of the smaller tracks, being sure to include a metal ruler in each picture for size reference.

The impression kit included: a one-gallon plastic bucket; a gallon jug of water; a box of dental stone; a can of hairspray; a can of cooking oil; some wooden tongue depressors for stirring the mixture; and some heavy duty plastic bags to hold the finished impressions. Because the soil was somewhat muddy, Rick first sprayed the tracks with the cooking oil, which served as a release agent. This would permit the cured impression to be removed without any debris clinging to it. Had the soil been sandy, he would have first used hairspray to firm up tracks before taking the impression.

He quickly mixed some of the dental stone with water, which produced a pancake-batter-like mixture that he carefully poured first around the outside of each track, and then into the most defined section of each. When sufficient time had elapsed (about thirty minutes), Rick carefully removed the casting and marked the back with a permanent marker to indicate the date and time of the collection, before placing each one in its own plastic bag.

Rick judged by the size of the tire tracks that it was a small car or pickup that had made them. It might not be helpful now, he thought, but would certainly be of assistance should a suspect be apprehended.

As he walked back to the Bronco, he chuckled at how boring most people would think this aspect of police work appeared. But it was simple procedure like this that helped catch so many criminals. Boring? Maybe. Effective? *Absolutely.*

He'd love to solve this one before Matt got back, but realistically the chances of that happening were slim and none — unless he got lucky.

Chapter 23

Montana

When Clint arrived home that evening, there was a second note in his mailbox. It was in an envelope this time, and the words "About Shorty" were typed on the outside. The note was also typewritten rather than written by hand. Clint read it carefully, several times. By the time he had finished reading it a third time, his eyes had grown moist with tears. The note read:

> *"Put the money in a plastic freezer bag and tape it with duck tape. Put it next to the gate at the entrance to your ranch. Do it at midnite tomorrow night. If theres anybody there when we come to pick it up, Shorty dies. Oh and we changed our mind. We want $75,000 or else. Once we have the money you get Shorty. Remember no funny buziness or Shorty dies."*

What in God's name do these people want from me?

Clint's hands were shaking almost uncontrollably as he folded the note and stuffed it into the envelope.

He called Ralph immediately.

Clint's voice was filled with alarm as he informed his friend, "Ralph, I got another note."

"What's it say?"

"They want more money than they did before."

"How *much* more?"

"Seventy-five thousand."

"Seventy-five *more*?"

"No, seventy-five altogether. And they want it by tomorrow night at midnight. What am going to do, Ralph? I don't have that kind of money. Hell I don't even have *forty* thousand. I'm scared, Ralph. I'm really scared. Sweet Jesus, if anything happens to Shorty, I'll never forgive myself."

"So what're you gonna do?"

"I . . . don't . . . know," Clint said slowly, emphasizing each word in turn.

"I'm coming over," Ralph offered. "I'll be there in ten minutes."

Ralph studied the note carefully. Whoever had typed it must have been the same person who wrote the original note, he observed. The same words were misspelled, and even though they looked less grammatically incorrect in typewritten form, their impact was the same. It was clear they needed to act and act now.

The two men sat quietly across from one another at the large, wooden table in Clint's kitchen. It was so quiet that the soft noise from the refrigerator sounded like the powerful hum of a high-power transmission line, and the *tick, tock, tick, tock* of the old grandfather clock standing in the corner mimicked the percussion section of a small band.

"I have an idea," Ralph announced, breaking the silence. "How much cash can you get your hands on?"

Clint leaned forward. "Five, maybe ten thousand at the most. I always try to have somewhere around that much in my checking account. You know, to pay my hands, buy feed, groceries, that kind of thing. It'd take me at least a week to get seventy five thousand together—that is, *if* I could even get that much. I'd have to talk to my banker, maybe take out some more paper on the ranch. The only other way I could get it is to rob a bank."

"Well that's not gonna happen," Ralph laughed. "Okay, let's start with five. Can you get five thousand cash first thing in the morning?"

"Sure. But what good will *that* do? I'm afraid I don't understand. They *want* forty."

"Stop and think about it. These fellers, whoever they are, only asked for forty thousand the first time, right?"

Clint nodded.

"Okay. So this isn't some high-powered bunch of professionals we're talkin' about. Just looking at the note tells us that. These fellers are a bunch of yokels, out to make a quick buck. Five thousand dollars is probably a lot of money to them."

"I see what you mean."

"Remember that movie with Jeff Bridges? You know, the one about the *nihilists*. Oh . . . what the hell was the name of that movie?" Ralph scratched his head. "You know the one. Phillip Seymour Hoffman played that sissy assistant. The Big Lebowski! *That's* it! Funny as hell. This crazy bunch of assholes were trying to extort money from some millionaire—the guy in the wheelchair—the *real* Lebowski. I mean, Jeff Bridges was also Lebowski, but—"

"Ralph!" Clint yelled. "What the *hell* are you talking about?"

"Oh, nothing. Forget it. I was just trying to . . . oh, hell, all I meant was that these guys kind of remind me of that bunch. In the end, the whole thing kind of fell apart. Really funny movie, though."

"I'm sure it was," Clint allowed. "But can we just stick to the situation at hand? Please?"

"Sure," Ralph apologized. "I'm sorry. I guess I just got kind of carried away. Okay, where were we? Oh yeah, the money."

"Right. The money," repeated Clint. "You said if I could just get five or ten thousand it'd be helpful."

"The point is," Ralph suggested, "it'll be enough to buy us some time. Also, once they've got some cash in their hands, they'll realize it'd be stupid to do anything to stop the flow. Shorty will be safe—at least for a while."

"Okay," admitted Clint, "I'll get down to the bank first thing in the morning and get the money."

"Good" Ralph replied. "Now give me the note and I'll show it to Matt and Chris as soon as I get back to the house. I'll run the whole thing by them. Don't worry, my friend, we're gonna get Shorty back and everything's gonna be A-Okay. I promise."

"I sure hope so."

"Talk to you in the morning."

Clint's dreams that night were the stuff of which movies are made—*horror* movies . . .

The bull was enormous. It wore a gold crown between its horns that had the name Tyrus engraved on it. The great beast aggressively pawed the dirt on the floor of a small paddock, kicking up huge clouds of dust. Shorty sat atop the animal on a red leather saddle decorated with bright gold stars along its edges, and was holding onto an enormous horn, which he gripped tightly with both hands. He had on a red felt, western hat and a red bandana. His long-sleeved western shirt was red, too, and was open at the neck, with mother of pearl buttons dotting the front. The fancy tooled boots he wore were colored claret, as were his jeans.

Suddenly, a small female cow appeared in the stall and presented herself to the bull. The bull reared up and tried to mount the female, but he couldn't because his sexual organ was missing. As a result, each time he attempted to mount her, his efforts were in vain.

Now, Shorty was screaming loudly, "Look! Look!" and pointing at the ground. There appeared to be something growing up out of the dirt like a mushroom; it was a gigantic male genitalia, and it was spurting blood everywhere.

A crowd of people materialized and they were screaming in unison, "Look at Shorty! Look at Shorty!"

Shorty was on the ground, astride a voluptuous, blond, naked woman. He had his jeans down around his ankles and was trying to enter the woman's vagina. But, like the bull, he had no sex organ. The woman had it in her hand.

"No! No!" cried Shorty. "Please don't take my pecker! Please! Please! Please! Not my pecker! Please . . ."

Clint awoke with a start, his breath ragged, and his heart beating wildly. "Oh Lord," he muttered. "Please be safe, Shorty. Please be okay." He got up, went into the bathroom, took a Xanax and two Advil tablets, and returned to bed. This time, his sleep was undisturbed, and he awoke with no memory of the hideous nightmare.

* * * * *

Matt and Chris took turns looking at the note. They agreed with Ralph that the same person who had written the original note had also typed the second. They listened attentively as Ralph explained his "plan."

"How did you arrive at the five thousand dollar figure?" Matt asked.

"Well," explained Ralph. "Like I told Clint, these guys remind me of that bunch of nihilists in that Jeff Bridges movie, The Big Lebowski—"

"Great flick," Chris said. "I must have seen it ten times, at least."

"What are nihilists?" asked Matt. He wasn't much of a movie fan, and had never seen the film.

"You know," replied Chris. "They're like . . . well . . . *nihilists*. They don't really *believe* in anything. They despise authority, civilization . . . pretty much everything."

"And they're not too bright" Ralph added, "especially that bunch in the movie. And I'm not too sure this group is any smarter. Five thousand just seemed like a nice round number. Not too big and not too small. Anyhow, the way I see it, if we give them a little money it'll kind of buy us some time . . . uh . . . that is until you fellers can figure out who they are and how we can rescue Shorty."

Matt and Chris sat quietly for a while, digesting everything Ralph had said. Finally, Matt addressed his concerns.

"It *sounds* like a good idea, Ralph. It really does. The only thing I'm worried about is, what if we're wrong? We're not talking about a movie here. This is real life, and these guys have already killed a valuable animal. Do we really want to take that chance with Shorty's life?"

Ralph frowned. "Well, I know what you mean, Matt. But what other choices do we have? I'm all ears. But I can tell you right now, Clint doesn't have seventy-five thousand dollars. Even five thousand is gonna be tough to spare."

Matt pursed his lips together. Ralph was right.

"By the way, did you fellers have any luck out there today?" Ralph asked, changing the focus of the conversation.

"Not really," admitted Chris. "We got a list of private hunting and fishing clubs from some gal over at Coldwell Banker, and we visited a few of them, but the people we spoke to there really weren't much help. They all seemed pretty closemouthed."

Matt added, "The rest of the day we checked out the local gun and tackle shops in the area. Pretty much the same result. Oh, there *was* one guy who had something kind of interesting to say."

"What was that?" asked Ralph.

"He seemed to have a real hard-on for the local Native American population. You know, the usual crap about how the *Injuns*, as he referred to them, have never gotten over the white man's manifest destiny—only he didn't quite say it so eloquently."

"Well, that's all well and good," Ralph replied. "Doesn't surprise me one bit. A lot of these locals think we should have wiped them *all* out, way back when, and been done with 'em all."

"And you?" Chris asked.

"Hell, I don't have anything against the Indians," Ralph confessed. "If anything, *they're* the ones who should complain. Anyway, that's yesterday's news. So what do you think about my plan?"

"I think it's a go," Chris offered. "Those kidnappers are expecting some money tomorrow night, and I don't think we ought to disappoint them. If they're *not* a bunch of jerks, then Shorty just might be in real danger—unless we can at least stall them."

Matt considered Chris's words. He had a point about the midnight deadline. There really *weren't* too many options. "Okay, Ralph," he agreed, "I guess your idea is as good as any. But we better be prepared for the worst."

Chris asked, "Did you say Clint was going to the bank in the morning?"

"Yep."

"Might be a good idea if we watch Clint from a distance while he makes the withdrawal," Matt said to Ralph. "See if anybody's watching him. I think these guys might actually *know* Clint—and *maybe* you, too. It'd be a good idea if you came with us and see if you recognize anybody who might look familiar."

Then he remembered Val.

"Hey, Ralph, you got a landline phone I can use?" He needed to call Val, if for no other reason than to let her know he was safe.

"Sure, do," replied Ralph. "There's a wall phone right there in the kitchen." He pointed in that direction. "I've only got two. One there and another in my bedroom—for emergencies."

"Frankly, I'm surprised you even have one at all," replied Matt. "These days, everybody's got a cell phone. Seems like landlines are a thing of the past. I'll bet in ten or twenty years they'll do away with them completely."

"I doubt it," countered Ralph. "Unless they start putting up more cell towers in a hurry. Reception ain't worth a damn here."

"Yeah," agreed Matt, "but that'll change. I remember just five years ago, you couldn't get a signal within five miles of Roscoe. Now, I can get one practically anywhere in the area."

Matt walked into the kitchen, picked up the handset of the wall phone, and was just about to dial when Ralph cautioned him, "Don't forget the time difference." He pointed at the large clock on the wall, which read ten fifteen.

Matt immediately returned the handset to its cradle. "Shit," he exclaimed. "It's a good thing you said that, Ralph. That's the last thing I need to do is scare the hell out of Val by calling her at—what—one in the morning?"

Ralph smiled. "No one likes *that* kind of a call."

"Yeah," agreed Matt. "I guess I'll have to remember to call her in the morning." He yawned and stretched his arms in the air. "Well, what do you say we get some shuteye, everybody," he suggested. "Tomorrow's going to be a long day."

That would turn out to be an understatement.

Chapter 24

Roscoe, NY

Al Coif watched the TV news broadcast with special attention. Usually, WICZ, FOX40, out of Binghamton, didn't pay much attention to local news originating out of the Roscoe area, but tonight they had made an exception.

Because the TV reception varied with the weather and how it affected the ancient antenna atop the old farmhouse, tonight's broadcast was not as good as it could be. But that didn't matter to Al, who watched the marginal image as though it were in HD. The cute little blond weather girl, who doubled as a waitress, was focused on a series of barn fires that had been reported over the last month, the most recent one occurring in Treadwell. Police and fire officials had declared that arson was definitely the cause of the blaze, but they had no suspects at the moment. The blond informed viewers that a thousand dollar reward had been offered by the owners of the affected property.

"Hot damn!" exclaimed Al, as he watched the contact information scroll across the screen. "I made the news." It never occurred to him that making the TV newscast might also mean that he stood a better chance of being caught. The truth was, when the urge struck — and it was striking far more frequently lately — it wouldn't have mattered if a string of police cars were surrounding his target. His compulsion gave new meaning to the phrase "burning a hole in my pocket." The more excitement he could generate, the better he liked it.

Al didn't *want* to get caught. He just could *not* stop himself from setting fires. In general, he was content with his life, living alone on the small dairy farm he had inherited when his mother passed away in 2010. The only time he experienced any feelings of pressure was at the end of each month when the bills came due. It was then that he was most inclined to accede to his weakness. That's when he missed the steadying influence of his late father and, now, of his deceased mother.

Most of the time, Al could limit his reaction to burning something harmless like leaves, or piles of brush. But when things were really tight, like now, with the economy in the doldrums and him being forced to do all of the necessary farm chores by himself; that's when things became most volatile.

Just that morning, a bill had come in the mail from the insurance company that covered his car and tractors. The premium had jumped almost fifty percent over the amount from the previous year's contract. Fortunately for Al, there was no mortgage on the property, but between the utilities, feed for the cows, fertilizer for the few crops he grew, and the cost of his own food, which had skyrocketed in recent years, Al found it difficult to make ends meet. The increase in the insurance premium just made things worse.

The TV news broadcast had ended by now, and Al turned off the set. He sat down in the frayed, upholstered rocker that his father had favored when he was alive, and closed his eyes, using his feet to rock gently to and fro, the rhythm of the movement soothing his anxiety. But nothing could keep him from worrying about the new financial obligation delivered in that morning's mail.

Finally, when he couldn't stop thinking about things, he got up and poured himself a beer, swilling it down in one, long, continuous swallow. He followed that with another, and another, and another, until the effects of the alcohol brought about the intended relief, and Al fell asleep in the rocking chair.

His last thought before succumbing to Hypnos was of the plastic gasoline container he'd carelessly left at the site of the burning barn, and whether or not it would lead the authorities back to him.

* * * * *

Rick Dawley never really wanted to be acting Chief of Police, but he couldn't very well say no when he was asked to assume the mantel. He was perfectly content to be a patrolman with no obligation to "The Job" once he was off duty, and certainly no responsibilities other than his daily patrol routine and following up on traffic citations and "drunk and disorderlies." Oh, there *had* been a few "real" crimes since he'd joined the force—even a murder of sorts—but the bulk of the responsibility for those cases had rested largely with Matt Davis.

But, like any police officer worth his salt, Rick didn't shirk responsibility once it had been made his own. So, with Matt out of town, the recent spate of arsons was weighing heavily on his mind. His main concern was that, sooner or later, someone was going to be hurt—or, worse yet, killed.

Later that morning, Rick searched several online databases containing reference files of tire treads to determine the brand/model of the tire that made the marks at the scene of the barn fire. The good news was that he found out that the tread was that of a 155/80R13 79T manufactured by Kumho, a Japanese newcomer to the tire industry.

He contacted the tire's manufacturer to determine which, if any, cars used that particular tire as standard equipment. To his dismay, he was informed that there were at least a dozen compact cars that fit the bill, not to mention the myriad of used cars that also could use that particular tire.

"Shit," Rick murmured, covering the mouthpiece on the phone, "why do I always get a warped one?" (He was referring to a line spoken by Mel Brooks in one of his favorite films, *Blazing Saddles*.) Still, he reasoned, it narrowed the list of suspect vehicles somewhat, and pretty much eliminated quite a few others.

"I'm sorry," said the person on the other end of the line, "did you say something?"

"Oh, no," explained Rick, "I was talking to someone else. Could you possibly email me that information as an attachment?"

"I'd be more than happy to," replied the woman."

Rick thanked her for her time and hung up.

When he received the email, he downloaded the attachment, printed the document, and placed the piece of paper in a manila folder he had labeled, "Arson Investigation - 2016." He made a mental note to keep his eyes open for any suspicious looking compact cars.

Yeah, right. Rotsa ruck with that one.

Chapter 25

Montana

All four of the kidnappers were sitting around the drop-leaf table in the kitchen area of the trailer. The talk was animated, and each one had a different take on the prisoner and what should be done with him.

"I think he's sympathetic with us," suggested Henry Golden Eagle.

"Yeah," agreed Jimmy Blackwater, "he understands what it's like for us in the white man's world."

Ronald White Feather disagreed. "He's just *playing* us, waiting for a chance to try to escape. I don't trust him."

Walter Begay pounded his fist on the Formica surface of the table. "Okay, okay, shut the hell up!" he ordered the other three men. "We've got business to attend to here. Tonight's when we get our money, and I need someone to make the pickup at the white man's ranch."

Each of the remaining three men looked at the other two, but no one made a move to volunteer.

"Come on, boys," Walter said, "We're all in this together. Now, who's it going to be? Henry? Ronald?"

The two younger men looked at one another and shrugged their shoulders.

"Not me," said Henry.

"Me either," affirmed Ronald.

"What about you, Jimmy?" Walter asked. "It better be one of you three, because I'm too damned old. Besides, I already done my part by putting this whole thing together and dropping off the second note. So how about it, who's it gonna be?"

At last, Jimmy raised his hand in slow motion. "I guess I can do it," he acknowledged. "But what if they're waiting for me? What if I get caught? They'll catch all of us."

"That's not gonna happen," Henry offered. "That man we've got in the back room is their best ranch hand. Hell, he's the *foreman*. They *need* him to run the ranch. The white men care about their workers—*almost* as much as they care about their stupid bulls. They're really dumb that way. I'll bet that old man cried his eyes out when he found that bull with his pecker cut off."

The others laughed.

"All right, let's get serious," Walter advised. "They're supposed to leave the money at midnight, which means that's probably when they figure we'll pick it up. If we go then, there's a good chance somebody will be waiting for us."

"Then when do we get the money?" asked Jimmy.

"We don't—"

"But—"

"At least *not* at midnight," Walter explained. "They'll hang around for a while, but when nobody shows up, they'll figure we got cold feet and they'll leave. *That's* when you'll go get the money."

Jimmy seemed perplexed. "But what if they take the money with them?"

"They won't," Walter replied. "They can't take that chance."

"So how am I going to get the money?"

Walter explained, "You'll walk right up to the gate, pick it up and walk back."

"All the way from here?"

"No, no, you idiot," laughed Walter. "No wonder the white man has so little respect for us. I'll *drive* you to within a half mile or so of the gate to the ranch—the same place where I parked when I dropped off the last note. There's a nice little rise, and we ought to be able to see everything that goes on from there."

"How're you gonna do that?" inquired Ronald. "It'll be dark."

Walter rolled his eyes and lifted his hands from his lap. He held aloft a pair of binoculars colored in a camouflage pattern. "That's what *these* are for," he explained. "They're Army surplus, night vision binoculars. Just like they used in Operation Desert Storm. Just forty-nine, ninety-nine on Amazon.com." He smiled broadly.

All three of the other men said in unison, "Ooooooh," before bursting into laughter.

"Okay. Here's what we're going to do," Walter announced. "Ronald and Henry, you'll stay with our prisoner. Somewhere around eleven thirty, Jimmy and me will drive to the spot and park. We'll watch the gate and wait until they drop off the money. When we're sure they've gone, we'll wait another half hour—just to be safe—and then Jimmy will go and get the money."

The others nodded in agreement.

"So, once we have the money, we'll let Shorty go, right?" It was Henry asking the obvious question.

Walter didn't utter a syllable, but sat stone-faced.

"Right? I mean, that *was* the deal. *We* get the money, *they* get Shorty back."

Silence from Walter.

"*Right*?" insisted Henry.

"We'll see," Walter finally said. "We'll just see."

Henry didn't like the tone of Walter's voice.

Back in the rear bedroom, Shorty, who had been listening intently to the animated conversation, felt his heart skip a beat at the last sentence Walter spoke.

He didn't like the tone of Walter's voice either.

The three younger men were asleep in the small living room area of the trailer, when, around eleven o'clock, Walter shook each of them awake.

"Okay," he said, "It's game time."

One by one, the others opened their eyes and stretched like cats after a nap. And, much like their feline counterparts, each was fully awake within seconds.

"Ronald," ordered Walter, "go check on the prisoner, and make sure he's secure. And be sure to lock the door behind you when you leave the room."

Ronald started toward the rear of the trailer.

"Henry, you'll stay here with Ronald. Jimmy and me should be back within an hour and a half—"

"And if you're not?"

Walter hesitated. "Well, then . . . I guess you're on your own."

"What's *that* supposed to mean?"

"Just what I said. You're on your own. You and Ronald will have to figure it out for yourselves."

"Great!"

"What are you worrying about?" Walter asked. "Everything is going to be fine. Just fine. They want their man back just as bad as we want to be rid of him. We'll figure out what to do with Shorty once we've got the money. Okay?"

Henry stood there with his mouth open.

"O-K?" repeated Walter.

"Yeah, sure," agreed Henry, without the slightest bit of conviction. "I guess so."

"Good," said Walter. He shouted down the hall, "Ronald! Everything okay with the prisoner?"

Ronald came walking toward the living room from the rear of the trailer. "Yeah," he informed Walter, "everything's just dandy. He's asleep."

"Did you lock the door?"

"Yep."

"Good. Okay, Jimmy, let's go get some money."

Chapter 26

Going to the bank to get the money had been uneventful. Matt and Chris had remained in the rental car, watching carefully to see if anyone followed Clint inside after he exited his truck.

"Make sure you ask for new bills," Matt had advised the rancher, when they had discussed the plan. "We'll copy down the serial numbers before you put them in the bag, so at least we'll be able to identify the money if we ever apprehend anyone. Remember, nothing bigger than a fifty."

The little bit of advice he'd offered hadn't been much consolation, and Matt knew it. But he had nothing more to suggest.

Many people came and went during the transaction, but no one stood out as suspicious. There were men and women of all ages, whites and Native Americans. But none of them did anything to distinguish themselves from anyone else.

Chris had been less than optimistic when he had remarked, "It's like looking for a friggin' needle in a haystack," which had only served to reinforce the hopeless atmosphere surrounding the situation.

His assessment was far more accurate than anyone wished to admit.

*   *   *   *   *

The moon was full, and the shadows it cast were as crisp as the edges of a newly minted twenty-dollar bill. And that was exactly what was stacked on the kitchen table—mostly twenties with a handful of fifties thrown in for good measure—five thousand dollars worth, in all. Clint hastily scrawled a note on a piece of paper. It read:

"To whom it may concern,

I need more time. Please don't hurt Shorty. Here's $5,000. It's all I had on hand. I'm trying to raise the rest of the money, but I need more time. Please let me know Shorty is okay.

Clint Davidson"

The rancher was tired and more than ready to make the drop. He folded the note and placed it in an envelope, then inserted the envelope into the freezer bag. He carefully taped the top of the plastic bag with grey duct tape, as he had been instructed to do in the typewritten ransom note. He looked around the kitchen, his eyes searching for *something*. Clint didn't know what he was looking for, but for some reason he felt he needed to be sure he hadn't overlooked anything. In reality, he was just stalling for time before he had to make the delivery. He had a bad feeling about the whole thing, and although he had no memory of the previous night's dream, his imagination was more than a match for its contents.

Ralph had offered to go with Clint to make the drop, but Clint had declined. "I don't want to take any chances," he had told his friend. "If I screw this up, it's on me. I don't want anybody else to have it on their conscience. I hope you understand, Ralph."

There had been no disagreement. Good friends knew when to concede.

Matt and Chris had made no such promise, however, and, unbeknownst to Clint, had positioned themselves about a quarter mile away from the entrance to the ranch, in a location that permitted them a full view of the gate, their rental vehicle hidden from site behind some brush.

Now, as he prepared to make the drop, Clint wished he hadn't been so hasty in declining his friend's offer of assistance.

"Screw it," he muttered, "it is what it is," and he headed out the door.

* * * * *

It was nearly a ten-minute drive to the entrance to the ranch, and Clint drove slowly, numb with fear, and not really believing what he was doing. He could only imagine the fear Shorty must be experiencing—*if* he was still alive. The possibility that he had been killed had crossed Clint's mind many times since the whole affair had begun. He comforted himself with the knowledge that nothing he had done so far could have possibly been done differently.

* * * * *

"What the fuck?" Walter Begay whispered. He was incredulous. In spite of the warning he had included in the last note, someone was driving past them in a bright new SUV. He watched as they drove past the gate and turned off the road about a quarter of a mile past the drop-off location. Because the night was so still, he could hear when they turned off the engine. Whoever was in that vehicle was probably waiting for them to pick up the money.

"Can you believe this shit?" he whispered

Jimmy Blackwater felt a chill run down his spine. "Maybe this ain't such a good idea after all."

"Oh shut up. It's okay. Better we know where they are then we don't."

Walter looked at his wristwatch. The digital readout displayed: 12:47 AM. *Not exactly the time for a drive in the country*, he thought. *That's okay. We'll just wait them out.*

"What're we gonna do?" asked Jimmy.

Walter verbalized his thoughts.

"But for how long?"

"As long as it takes."

* * * * *

Chris was almost asleep, his mind in that nether land where reality mixes with imagination. Matt's whispered voice broke the silence. "It's two fifteen. I don't think they're going to show."

"Yeah," Chris agreed. "I think you're right. It was probably a test to see if anybody was watching."

"These guys are a lot cagier than I expected," Matt acknowledged. "Let's give it another fifteen minutes and we'll call it a night."

"More like a morning," Chris quipped.

Exactly fifteen minutes later, the two men agreed to call it quits, and drove the ten miles or so back to Big Sky Fin and Fur, passing within five hundred feet of two of the kidnappers.

*　*　*　*　*

Walter roused Jimmy Blackwater from a deep sleep and informed him, "They've left. Get moving!"

"What time is it?" asked the sleepy-eyed Jimmy.

"Never mind that," barked Walter. "It's time to go."

Jimmy blinked several times, opened the door of the pickup, and started for the ranch entrance. "Wish me luck," he called over his shoulder.

"Just go," Walter replied.

Less than twenty minutes later, the young Indian returned with the plastic bag, wearing a big smile. "I got it," he proudly announced.

"Good," Walter said, snatching the surprisingly light bag from his accomplice. "Now let's get the hell out of here."

Chapter 27

Bobcat Walker and Pete Richards, the two other patrolmen on the Roscoe police force, were comparing notes on the recent spate of barn fires.

"What do you think, Pete?" inquired Bobcat. "Is it some nut job, or somebody using the fires as a distraction?"

"What kind of distraction?"

"Well, maybe while the fire's burning, the perp is ransacking the residence, looking for . . . well . . . anything of value, I guess. Jewelry, money . . . I don't know, stuff."

"Nah," replied Pete. "No one's reported anything missing. And don't forget, the last fire was a barn that was standing all alone. Nope. I think he's just one sick bastard, someone who gets his jollies watching things go up in smoke. And that's what makes it so hard. Other than the little men running around inside this guy's head telling him what to burn, there's no motive."

Bobcat laughed at his partner's imagery. "I like it," he said. "Little men inside the guy's head. Cute. Probably green, too."

Just then, Rick Dawley appeared in the doorway of the office shared by the other two.

"I've been thinking," he said. "It would be a good idea to start asking around the area service stations to see if anyone recalls filling up plastic gas cans for anybody recently."

Bobcat shook his head. "Good luck with that."

Rick looked at him quizzically.

"There are only two states in the union that prohibit customers from pumping their own gas—and we ain't one of 'em."

Rick smiled. "You're right," he conceded. "I guess I've gotten spoiled." Whether it was out of deference to the badge, or just a local courtesy, Rick had never been asked to fill his own gas tank, ever since being sworn in as a patrolman. Some customs just died hard, especially in a rural area like Roscoe.

Bobcat suggested, "We could still question service station attendants in the area, and ask whether they remember anyone filling up a bunch of gas containers recently."

Now, it was Rick who was shaking his head.

Bobcat shrugged his shoulders. "Okay, okay. It's a long shot, I grant you that. But, who knows, maybe our guy has a thing about not pumping his own gas. It's worth asking, don't you think?"

"I suppose it couldn't hurt," Rick conceded.

Bobcat grinned.

"But it'd be a hell of a long shot," Rick added.

Long shot? Hell, it'd be like winning the lottery.

But Rick knew he had to do whatever they could to apprehend the firebug terrorizing the local countryside.

The sooner Matt returned, the better Rick would like it.

Chapter 28

Montana

Walter burst through the front door of the doublewide, waving the freezer bag full of money in the air. Jimmy, elated and wearing a huge smile, followed closely behind the older man, his feet barely touching the ground.

Walter stopped dead in his tracks when he entered the living room. "What the —"

Ronald and Henry were fast asleep on the stained sectional in front of the fifty-inch flat screen TV. An infomercial for a male enhancement product may as well have been broadcasting its message into outer space for all the good it was doing.

Walter slapped Henry across the face. "Wake up!" he shouted. He repeated the process on Ronald with even greater vigor. "Jimmy, check the prisoner," he ordered. "And make sure to take the rifle with you."

By now, the two men on the couch were fully awake.

Henry rubbed his cheek where Walter had struck it.

"Christ, Walter, what'd you do that for?" An angry welt was already starting to show.

Ronald's face showed the full imprint of Walter's hand.

"You were supposed to be watching the prisoner," Walter barked, "not watching the fucking TV. When's the last time you checked on him?"

"Relax, Walter. We've been taking turns," Henry said.

"That's not the way it looked to me," Walter observed. "If that son of a bitch is gone, you two will be the ones chasing his ass."

Just then, Jimmy came walking up the hall, the Henry rifle cradled in his arms. "It's okay," he advised Walter. "He's right where he oughta be—in bed and asleep. I checked the handcuffs and everything is fine."

"*This* time, maybe," grumbled Walter. "But next time we might not be so lucky."

Jimmy placed the rifle against the wall in the corner of the room nearest the TV. "How about it, Walter, we gonna open the bag?" He rubbed his hands together like someone preparing for a feast.

Walter smiled and sat down at the head of the drop-leaf table. "Okay, okay, everybody come sit down. Let's see what seventy-five thousand dollars looks like. Jimmy hand me a knife."

Jimmy extracted a Buck 110 Folding Hunter from the leather carrying case he wore strapped to his belt; he never went anywhere without it. "Here," he said, offering it to Walter, along with a broad smile. "Just watch your fingers. I just honed that son of a bitch, and she's sharp as a razor."

Walter reached out and yanked the knife from Jimmy's outstretched hand. "Don't tell *me* how to handle a knife. I was slicing and dicing before you were born." He carefully unfolded the knife and smiled when the blade snapped into place with a crisp *thwack.* He held the freezer bag in his left hand and carefully inserted the tip of the Buck under the edge of the duct tape. With a slow and steady pressure, he began cutting the tape until the bag was completely open.

"Let's see it," Jimmy urged. "I never seen that much money. I can't wait to touch it."

Walter turned the bag upside down and unceremoniously dumped its contents onto the middle of the table. The sound it made was not very impressive. In addition to the money there was an envelope.

"Looks like a note," observed Ronald.

Walter rolled his eyes and opened the envelope. He removed the piece of paper from within the bag, unfolded it, and began to read the note aloud. "To whom it may concern. I need more time —"

"More time?!" yelled Ronald.

Walter's eyes narrowed as he continued reading the note. "Please don't hurt Shorty. Here's five thousand dollars —"

"*Five* thousand dollars!" shouted Jimmy. "What happened to the other *seventy*?"

Walter continued reading, but no one was paying any attention. It was as if all the air had gone out of the room. When he'd finished, he let the paper drop from his hand and onto the pile of money, where it landed without a sound.

"Son . . . of . . . a . . . bitch," he said slowly, emphasizing each word. "Who the hell does he think he is? That son of a bitch has got every dime he ever made. I'm *sure* of it. If he thinks he can get away with this, I'll —"

"You'll what?" asked Henry. "What are you going to do, Walter? This whole thing was your big idea. Now what?"

Walter had no answer.

"That's what I thought," observed Ronald. "You don't know *what* to do. Well *I* know what we ought to do. We ought to do exactly what we said we would. Cut the man's pecker off and send it to Davidson in a jar."

Henry sat quietly and listened as the other two younger men went at Walter, who, for once, seemed unable to command their respect. They accused him of not thinking the plan through, of being greedy, of putting all of them in danger. For his part, Walter argued that no one could have ever foreseen what had happened.

"Are we done?" Henry asked softly, his voice tinged with a determined anger. "Are you all finished with your bullshit arguing?"

The other three men looked at him in shock. Henry had always been the quietest of the bunch, pretty much going along with anything they proposed. Now, however, his words were confrontational and challenging.

"What's on your mind, Henry Golden Eagle?" Walter inquired.

When Walter used Henry's full Indian name, Henry knew he was serious—*and* that he was paying attention. But now there was a deferential tone to the older man's voice. And that pleased Henry.

"I think you are all missing the point," he began.

"What point?" asked Ronald.

"This may not be the end of the line," Henry continued. "Maybe it's just the beginning."

"What the hell are you talking about?" inquired Jimmy.

Walter held up his right hand. "Wait, wait. I think I know what he means."

Henry smiled. *Walter isn't as dumb as I thought.*

Walter continued. "We'll *get* the seventy-five thousand — eventually. It'll just take a little longer than we thought. Right, Henry?"

"That's right," Henry affirmed. "And, if we play our cards right, that old *bull* we killed just might turn out to be — drum roll, please — a genuine cash *cow!*"

"Eggggggzactly!" Ronald exclaimed. "So let's forget about cutting off anybody's pecker, and start figuring out our next move. How about it, Walter? How's that sound?"

"Sounds like a plan."

Henry breathed a sigh of relief.

As a kind of incentive, Walter gave each of the other men a couple of crisp fifty-dollar bills. "Don't spend it all in one place," he laughed.

* * * * *

Back in the rear of the trailer, Shorty wasn't taking any chances. He was making plans of his own.

Chapter 29

Roscoe, NY

Nancy Cooper sat at her desk, quietly contemplating her future—or what little there might be of it. She wasn't getting any younger. The secretary had been with the Roscoe Police Department for most of her working days, but the time was drawing near for retirement. Thanks to a discreet erasure on her employment application, no one knew her exact age, and that was how she preferred it.

A single woman all her life, Nancy had no blood relative with which to share her retirement years, but she did have lots of old friends. The problem was they were all *really* old. She needed to find someone to accompany her on whatever traveling she might decide to do. One trip she definitely intended to make was to England, the land of her ancestors.

According to an entry on a website she had visited, the Cooper surname was an "occupational name" for a maker and repairer of wooden vessels such as barrels, tubs, buckets, casks, and vats, from Middle English *couper*, or *cowper* which was derived from Middle Dutch and so forth. Her eyes had nearly crossed when she read the full etymological explanation.

Bottom line: she wanted to see England.

The other dilemma facing Nancy was that of when to officially call it quits. She supposed the neatest way to wrap it all up was to make it official as of December 31st. That would give her from January through the end of April to find a companion and to plan the trip, which she hoped to take in July or August. She belonged to several women's groups, and her search to find a travel partner would most likely start there.

"What're you up to, Nancy?" It was Bobcat.

"Oh, nothing," she replied. "Just contemplating my future."

"Well that doesn't sound like *nothing* to me." He added, "Especially for a young woman like you."

"Okay, okay, what do you want? And don't say nothing." Nancy knew Bobcat like a book. Along with the flattery there usually was an ulterior motive.

Bobcat shook his head side to side, conceding defeat. "Alright, you got me," he admitted. "I need you to make about fifty copies of this notice I just made up." He handed her a piece of paper. Nancy studied its contents. It was a notice asking the public's assistance in identifying the person or persons guilty of setting the most recent barn fire, and offering a small reward for information leading to that person's arrest and conviction.

"Do you really think this will do any good?" Nancy inquired of the patrolman.

"I don't know," Bobcat answered, "but Rick asked me to write it, so I did. One thing's for sure. If we don't find this nut job soon, somebody's bound to be hurt, or, worse yet, killed. These things always seem to escalate."

"Well," Nancy said, "It would be nice if you fellows could find whoever did it before Matt gets back from Montana. That poor man's got more balls in the air than a circus juggler."

"You can say that again," quipped Bobcat.

"Okay," replied Nancy. "That poor man's got—"

Bobcat held up his right hand in the classic "stop" position, and Nancy complied immediately.

"I'll have your copies ready after lunch," Nancy informed him. "Speaking of which, I heard that new Mediterranean restaurant over on Stewart Avenue is selling *falafel*. I've always wanted to try something exotic like that. I have no idea what it is, but everybody seems to like it—at least those folks who come from the city."

"I've never had it," admitted Bobcat. "But, what the hey, how bad could it be? Do you want company?"

"I thought you'd never ask," Nancy replied, with a sparkle in her eye. "How's about in half an hour? We can walk over together."

"Okay. Sounds good."

Nancy noted Bobcat's expanding waistline and added, "Walk would probably do you good."

Bobcat frowned in mock embarrassment, then patted his stomach. "Couldn't hurt, I guess. I'll see you at noon."

*   *   *   *   *

Nineteen-year-old Bruce Pfeffer had been hitchhiking for two days. His journey had started just outside Rochester, at the edge of the Rochester Institute of

Technology campus. His destination was New York City, where he intended to meet up with his old high school sweetheart, who had invited him down for a Jason Mraz concert. He'd spent the first night at a campground, just outside Endicott. The owner had charged him five dollars to sleep on a couch in the little rec room across from the rest rooms. It wasn't the best night's sleep Bruce ever had (the little electric heater made just enough noise to all but eliminate the possibility of any REM sleep), but it *did* save him from paying for a motel room.

The last ride he caught had deposited him on State Highway 206, halfway between Downsville and Roscoe, at the mouth of Spring Brook Estates Road.

"This is as far as I go," the elderly driver of the car had apologized. "I live right up this road. But you're only a couple of miles from Roscoe now, and you can pick up Route Seventeen right in town by the diner. Should be easy to catch a ride into the city from there. It's only a couple of hours away."

Bruce thanked the man, and then began walking southeast toward Roscoe. It was fast approaching eleven o'clock, and the young college student was tired. He reached into the backpack he was carrying and extracted a granola bar and a half-filled bottle of water. The high carbohydrate content of the granola quieted his hunger, and the lukewarm water, although not particularly refreshing, slaked his immediate thirst. The combination of drink and food also made him sleepy.

Screw it, he thought. *I've got two days before the concert. I need some rest.*

Up ahead was a side road, and when he got to the intersection, he saw an old barn in the distance, perhaps a quarter mile down the road.

The hay's in the barn, he thought, recalling something one of his high school teachers used to say. *Maybe I can get some shuteye in there.* He picked up his pace, and, within five minutes, he had reached his temporary destination. The ancient structure was surrounded by a large cornfield, but there wasn't another building in sight.

Perfect.

Bruce approached the barn cautiously and opened one of the two doors. The place was empty, but there wasn't any hay to lie on. *Shit.* There was nothing but a dirt floor. He turned on the flashlight app on his iPhone and moved its beam around the interior of the barn. In the far left corner, there were several discarded burlap sacks that he could fashion into a kind of bed, and a heavy canvas tarp that would make an excellent blanket. He closed the door behind him, and, using the light from the iPhone, made his way into the corner. Within minutes, he had burrowed beneath the tarp, his head resting on the makeshift pillow of the backpack, and five minutes later he was fast asleep.

*　*　*　*　*

It was just past ten in the evening when Al Coif pulled the Datsun into the Sunoco filling station next to the Walton Diner, grabbed the three empty gasoline containers from off the backseat, and walked inside.

"How about filling these up?" he asked the pimply faced clerk, handing him the empty containers. "And let me have one of those hot dogs." He pointed at the contraption with the revolving stainless steel rollers that cooked the reddish-colored pieces of prepared meat. "Better make it two," he added.

The clerk stood rooted behind the cash register.

"Well," Al asked, "aren't you gonna fill these up for me?"

"No, sir. Gotta stay inside the store. It's self serve, here, you know."

Al shook his head and walked over to the bank of glass refrigerator doors lining the far wall and extracted a six-pack of Yuengling beer in bottles from one of the compartments. The clerk was just putting the two hot dogs into the buns by the time Al returned to the counter. He handed the hot dogs to Al, who spooned some mustard, relish, and raw onions on each.

"Will there be anything else?" asked the clerk.

"Yeah. You can fill these gas cans."

"Sorry. No can do."

"Oh, for god's sake," hissed Al, handing the kid a twenty dollar bill. "Take out what I owe you for the hot dogs and beer."

"What about the gas?"

"I'll pay you for the gas *after* I fill up the containers."

Al quickly gobbled down one of the hot dogs, then the other. "Watch my beer," he said. "I'll be right back."

He picked up the three gasoline containers from off the floor and headed out the door.

When he returned, he paid the attendant, retrieved his beer and left. It was just a short drive from the service station, back over the mountain to the barn he had targeted. Once he was on the main highway, Al unscrewed the cap from a bottle of beer and began drinking—*and* driving.

*　*　*　*　*

Not more than half an hour later, Bobcat Walker parked his vehicle in front of the same Sunoco station and walked inside. He flashed his badge at the teenager behind the counter and showed him one of the flyers Nancy had printed up. He could still taste the garlic from the falafel he'd eaten at lunch. Different, he had concluded, but not bad.

"I was wondering if you might tack this up on your little bulletin board over there?" Bobcat asked, pointing to a cork-surfaced bulletin board behind the clerk.

"I'll have to get permission from the owner," the young man replied, paying little attention to the contents of the flyer. His disinterested attitude was typical of most young people, concluded Bobcat. If it wasn't connected to a pair of speakers, it wasn't worth paying attention to.

"Do what you have to do," Bobcat advised, "but I'd sure appreciate it if you'd put it up as soon as possible."

The clerk accepted the piece of paper from Bobcat, quickly scanned its contents, and handed it back. Then, something clicked. "Hey!" exclaimed the clerk, "There was a guy in here just a little while ago with some gas cans. He wanted *me* to fill 'em up for him. Imagine that."

"What'd he look like?"

"Oh, wow, I really wasn't paying much attention."

No shit, Sherlock.

"Young? Old? White? Black? Hispanic?" inquired Bobcat.

"White guy," the clerk replied. "Got a couple of hot dogs — and a six-pack of Yuengling."

"How old was he?"

The kid rolled his eyes. "I don't know. Middle aged. Like you, I guess."

Bobcat wasn't quite sure how to take that.

"What kind of car was he driving?"

The clerk closed his eyes, in an apparent attempt to conjure up an image of the vehicle.

"It was blue," he said, in a voice brimming with pride. "Yeah, it was definitely blue."

"That's it, huh? That's all you remember?"

"Hey, I'm sorry, man . . . uh . . . officer. I just sell gas. I didn't know there'd be a quiz."

Wise ass.

It was apparent to Bobcat that he wasn't going to get any information from the attendant. He handed the kid one of his cards. "If you remember anything else, give me a call, okay?"

The clerk studied the card, then turned around and thumbtacked it to the crude bulletin board on the wall.

"Here," said Bobcat, "put this up there while you're at it." He handed him the flyer.

The young man hesitated.

"Come on. It's okay," Bobcat assured him. "You're boss won't give a crap one way or the other. I guarantee it."

"Yeah, but—"

"And you might save somebody's life."

"But—"

"I'd really appreciate it."

"Okay, but if I get in trouble . . ."

Bobcat turned to walk away. Over his shoulder he said, "You won't. Thanks, kid."

As he walked back to his vehicle, Bobcat thought about how much the world had changed—and not for the better.

Chapter 30

Montana

Matt punched in his home number on the keypad of the wall phone in Ralph's kitchen and held the receiver to his ear. It was just past six in the morning in Montana, or around nine in New York State in the Eastern Standard time zone. It was a good time to catch Val before she started her day.

He tapped his foot impatiently as he listened to the ring count reach two, then three, then four, until finally there was a click and Val's welcoming voice could be heard on the other end of the line.

"Hello?"

Matt breathed a sigh of relief. "Hi, honey. It's me."

"Matt!" exclaimed Val. "Thank goodness. I was beginning to worry."

"I'm sorry, Val. The damned cell phone is all but useless here. This is 'Big Sky Country,' and, boy, they're not kidding." Then, he added, "Big sky, no reception."

A pregnant pause, then, "So, how are you?" Val asked.

"Good. Good. *Really.* I'm fine. I'm just glad I caught you. It never occurred to me until yesterday—last night, actually—that I could use a landline . . . and then, it was after midnight . . . and anyway that's why I waited until this morning."

"It's okay, Matt. Really. I understand. It's just nice to hear your voice."

"Yours too."

"Are you having any luck?"

"I wish I could say yes, but actually we're not having much luck at all. I don't know if I've ever been so damned frustrated. If this were a *normal* case, we could be doing so much more. But our hands are tied. So, to answer your question, no, we're not."

Matt closed his eyes, visualizing his wife's face. He hated not being there with her. Ever since her bout with breast cancer, he'd felt a need to spend more time with her—just in case.

"Matt, are you still there?"

"Yeah, yeah. I'm still here."

Matt was thinking how comforting it was just to hear Val's voice. In spite of all the years they'd been married, he could still be reduced to the age of a high school boy by the sound of her sweet voice on the phone.

"So, what's new?" he asked.

"Not much, honey. Same old, same old."

"I knew that," Matt laughed. "I meant anything going on I should know about?"

"Well," Val informed him, "there *was* another barn fire, over in Treadwell."

"Anybody hurt?"

"No, thank God. But people are definitely getting worried."

"Can't say that I blame them," Matt agreed.

"You really ought to talk to Rick," Val suggested. "I talked to Nancy the other day, and she said he's doing fine, but he'd probably like to hear from you just the same."

"Believe me, I know," Matt said. "I mean I *know* I ought to call him. As soon as we're done, I'll—"

"Oh, there *is* one other thing," Val interrupted.

"What's that?"

"Nancy's retiring."

"What?! Where'd you hear that?"

"Bobcat."

"When?"

"Just the other day."

"No, no" Matt laughed. "I *meant* when is she retiring?"

"I'm not sure, but I think by the end of the year."

"Oh, great. Just what I don't need—especially now."

"Now, Matt," Val admonished him, "you knew she wasn't going to stay on forever."

"I know. It's just that—"

"You'll really miss her, won't you?"

"Miss her? Hell, I don't know what I'll do *without* her. Does anybody else know she's leaving?"

"Do you mean like the mayor?"

"Yes, I meant Harold. Does he know?"

"I don't think so. I imagine Nancy would want that to come from you. She said no one else was to know—except for you, Bobcat, Pete, and Rick, of course"

"I guess I knew it was inevitable, but boy, oh boy, I can't believe she's really going to leave."

"Speaking of leaving," Val said. "I hate to do this, honey, but I I'm afraid I have to go. I'm supposed to meet Cathy Emanuel over at the coffee shop at nine thirty."

Matt hated for their conversation to end. He wished this whole thing was over.

"Okay, honey. I really should go, too. I haven't spoken to Rick in . . . what's it been . . . four . . . no, five days already. Say hi to Cathy for me—and to anybody else who gives a damn."

"I love you, Matt," Val whispered.

"I love you, too, sweetheart."

Matt hung up the phone, then immediately picked it up again and dialed headquarters.

"Roscoe Police Department," said Nancy, in her most official sounding voice. How may I direct your call?"

"Well, I'm looking for a secretarial position for my wife," joked Matt. "Would you possibly have any openings?"

Without missing a beat, Nancy replied, "I'm sorry, sir, but all of our positions are filled—and by some really competent personnel. Is there anything else I can help you with?"

Matt smiled.

"Sir? Did you hear what I said?"

"Yes, yes," Matt laughed. "Okay, smarty, let me speak to Rick, will you, Nancy? Oh, and congratulations on your retirement."

"Thanks, Matt," Nancy replied. "I really wanted to tell you myself, but I guess *somebody* let the cat out of the bag."

"That's okay," Matt assured her. "We all know Bobcat is a little . . . shall we say . . . *challenged*."

"Did he tell you?"

"No, but he told Val, and Val told me."

"Well as long as he hasn't told Harold."

"Val says he hasn't."

"That's good," Nancy replied. "I'll get Rick on the line."

A moment later, Rick picked up.

"How's everything going in the great state of Montana, Matt?"

"It's *going* all right. Right down the tubes."

"That bad, huh?"

"Let's just say things are not going as smoothly as I'd hoped. I never realized how difficult this was going to be without being able to go through the usual channels."

"Sounds a bit like what's going on here," Rick informed him.

"Val told me there's been another fire. How many is that now, three?"

"Yep."

"That's three too many."

"Agreed."

"So what are you doing so far to catch this asshole?"

"Well, we know he's using gasoline as an accelerant, because State found an empty gas can at the Treadwell fire."

"Did they dust it for prints?"

"Yep. Came back negative."

"Okay. What else?"

"Well, we printed up a bunch of flyers asking anyone with any information to contact us immediately. In fact, Bobcat's running around Sullivan and Delaware Counties handing them out to all the gas stations now."

"Okay. That's a good start. Anything else?"

"Well, I took some tire impressions at the Treadwell crime scene, and I know we're looking for a small car, probably an import."

There was a brief pause, and then Matt said, "Well, stay on top of things. There probably isn't much more that you can be doing at this point. Looks like we're both in the same fix."

"Yeah," agreed Rick with a laugh, "but at least *you're* out in Montana."

"Actually, I'd rather be home," Matt confessed. "But I'm sure you're doing the best you can, and that's all I can ask. I'll check back with you in a couple of days."

"Sounds good. Talk to you then."

"Right."

Nothing *right* about any of it, Matt thought as he hung up the phone.

Chapter 31

Clint Davidson paced back and forth in his kitchen. He knew that the five thousand dollar down payment he'd made the night before would keep the kidnappers at bay for only so long. At some point, they needed to find out where Shorty was and try to rescue him—*if* he was still alive.

He picked up the phone and punched in Ralph's phone number. After a few rings, his friend answered.

"Hello. Big Sky Fin and Fur Resort."

"Ralph, it's me. Let me talk to Matt, will ya?"

"Well, good morning to you, too," Ralph replied. "I'm fine, thanks. And how are you?"

"I'm sorry," Clint apologized, "I didn't mean to be so rude. Forgive me, will ya, Ralph? I'm just plumb wore out with this whole mess. Are you doing all right?"

"Yeah, yeah, I'm doin' fine. It's okay. I was just busting your balls. I really *do* understand—*completely*. I *do*. *Honest*. Now let me get Matt on the line for you."

"Thanks."

"Not a problem, buddy."

A moment later, Clint heard Matt's voice.

Good morning, Clint. What's up?"

"How'd it go last night?" He wasn't wasting any time with petty formalities. "Did you learn anything?"

"Nope. We waited until nearly two, but they never showed."

"Well, *somebody* showed up," Clint informed Matt, "because the bag of money is gone."

"Shit! I knew we should have stayed longer," Matt admitted. "But I figured when they hadn't shown up by two, it was probably just a dry run to see if anyone was watching. Damn! I'm really sorry, Clint."

"It's okay," Clint said. "I would have done the same thing if I were you. That's ancient history now. So what do we do next? I'm sure I'm going to hear more from them soon."

"I'm sure you're right," Matt agreed. "Let me know as soon as you do, okay?"

"Will do."

"Good. We're going to start hitting all the bars in the area tonight. You know, ask some questions, see if anyone's been flashing a lot of money, or shooting off their mouths. In the meantime, we'll probably do some more fishing today—just in case we're being watched."

Clint was silent for a while, then said, "Yeah, it's a tough job, but *somebody's* gotta do it."

"Nice to see you haven't lost your sense of humor."

"Yeah, well. If I didn't have *that*, I don't know *what* I'd do. Is Ralph taking you out?"

"Uh huh."

"Well, at least you'll be in good hands. I'll talk to you tonight, I guess."

It wasn't more than an hour later when Clint's phone rang. He picked it up on the first ring. "Hello?"

"What kind of shit are you trying to pull, white man?"

Clint struggled to identify the voice on the other end of the line, but was drawing a blank.

"Did you *hear* what I said?" continued the man. "We asked for seventy-five thousand dollars, not *five*!" The man's voice was filled with rage. "What didn't you understand about the note? We're not fooling around, *white man*. Do you want your ranch hand back alive or don't you?"

"Yes, yes. Of course," Clint answered. "But I told you, I need more time."

"And we need more money! A *lot* more money."

"How do I know Shorty's even still alive?" Clint's mind was racing. He needed to keep this man on the line. Maybe he'd say something—*anything*—that would give a clue about who he was, or where he was.

"Listen, white man. If I give you proof, will you give us the money?"

There it was—*the clue*!

That was the third time the man had used the phrase "white man." Clint reasoned that only a Native American would be referring to him as white man.

He must be an Indian!

"You give me some proof that Shorty's still alive, and I'll see about getting you some more money. No proof, no money. That's it. Take it or leave it."

Clint knew he was taking a chance, but there didn't seem to be any other way forward. It was like a giant chess game, with Clint merely a pawn, and the other player holding all the major pieces. But right now, it was a stalemate of sorts, with Clint awaiting his opponent's next move.

"Okay, you'll get your proof," the voice on the other end of the line said. His tone seemed less cocky, more conciliatory.

"I'll be here."

Click. The phone went dead.

"Shit," Clint whispered, "I hope I haven't gone and screwed this whole thing up."

You hang in there, Shorty. You just hang in there.

His thoughts drifted off into space, just about as useless as he felt under the circumstances.

*   *   *   *   *

Shorty turned the worn dial on the little transistor radio as slowly as he could, trying to hone in on the only station it was capable of receiving. Above the static it made, he could hear the faint sound of two of his captors' voices coming from the far end of the double wide. Of course, he had no way of knowing what kind of building he was in, since he still had a blindfold across his eyes.

The talking stopped, and a moment later he heard the sound of the door opening and closing. Someone had entered the room. Shorty could smell the aroma of food. He hoped it wasn't another turkey TV dinner. He'd about had his fill of that crap.

"Hey, I brought you some chili," said Jimmy Blackwater. "I made it myself this morning. It's got fresh elk meat in it."

"Oh, thank God," Shorty replied, recognizing the voice of Injun Two. "If I had to eat another TV dinner, I think I'd kill myself." He turned off the radio and waited.

Jimmy Blackwater said nothing.

"Hey, what's your name, man?" Shorty inquired. Then, he went through the same routine he'd gone through with Ronald, about not wanting the man's last name, just his first name.

"Why should I tell you my name?" Jimmy asked.

Shorty replied, "Oh, no reason I guess. Hell, no reason at all. Never mind then, I guess I'll just keep thinking of you as Injun Two. Suit yourself."

"It's Jimmy!" replied the Indian. "And don't *ever* call me Injun again, or I swear I'll—"

"You'll what? Scalp me? I *know* you're a damn injun. You're *all* a damn bunch of injuns. Why—"

Smack! Jimmy struck the prisoner hard on his left cheek.

"*Ow! Damn it!* Okay, okay, take it easy. I went a little over the line. I'm sorry. No more *injun* talk, okay?"

Nothing.

I promise . . . okay . . . *Jimmy*."

Silence.

"I *said* I'm sorry," Shorty apologized. "Can I have the chili now?" He added, "I'm really hungry. I'm sorry. Honest."

"Hold out your hands," Jimmy ordered.

Shorty did as he was told. Jimmy placed the hot bowl of chili in his hands, cautioning him, "It's hot. Be careful."

"How about a spoon?"

"Hold your horses."

"I wish I *had* a damn horse," Shorty joked. "Then maybe I could get the hell out of here."

"Hold the bowl with your left hand," Jimmy said, ignoring the remark.

Shorty complied.

"Here's the spoon." Jimmy placed the utensil in Shorty's right hand. "Now eat," he commanded.

Shorty didn't answer; he just began shoveling the hot food into his mouth. In less than five minutes, he had devoured the entire bowlful. He burped loudly and said, "That's some pretty damn good chili, partner . . . er . . . Jimmy. Thanks, man."

Shorty felt the bowl and spoon being taken roughly from his hands. "I said that's some pretty good —"

"Here, drink this," Jimmy ordered, handing Shorty a metal cup filled with water.

Shorty held the cup to his mouth and eagerly drank its contents, trying hard not to spill any. It was a losing battle. He held out the cup again. "Can I get some more?"

Jimmy removed the cup from Shorty's outstretched hand without responding.

"I'll take that as a no," Shorty quipped.

"We'll see," replied Jimmy. "We'll see."

Later that afternoon, Walter entered the doublewide. Ronald was sitting on the couch in the living room, drinking a Mountain Dew, and munching Cheetos in front of the TV.

"Give me your iPhone," Walter said.

Ronald extracted the phone from his right front pocket and handed it to the older man. "Don't use all my data," he advised Walter.

Without answering, Walter turned and walked down the hallway to the room housing Shorty. He had Ronald's iPhone in one hand and a copy of that morning's edition of the *Montana Standard* in the other. Shorty was seated on the bed, propped up against the headboard, listening to the little transistor radio, his hands handcuffed in front of him in his lap.

Walter reached down, yanked the radio from Shorty's hand, and switched it off.

"Hey! What the —"

"Shut up, white man," Walter said.

He placed the newspaper, with the masthead facing front, in Shorty's lap.

"Hold this," Walter ordered. He reached out and guided Shorty's right hand to the top edge of the folded newspaper. "And don't move."

"What is it?" Shorty asked.

"Never mind that. Just hold it and don't move."

Walter focused the iPhone's camera on the subject, making sure that the newspaper's masthead was included in the frame.

"Say cheese," Walter said with a chuckle.

"Fuck you!"

"No, *cheese.*"

Walter then took a succession of pictures. He checked to make sure that the newspaper's date was visible in each, and satisfied that it was, removed the paper from Shorty's grasp.

Without saying another word, Walter left the room, locked the door behind him, and walked into Ronald's bedroom. He used the iPhone's Bluetooth to print a copy of the picture on the HP printer Ronald kept in his room, and then used the iPhone to call Shorty's boss.

"Hey, white man, your proof will be in an envelope by the gate tonight," Walter told Clint. "Check for it around midnight. And remember, no funny stuff. If I see *anybody* within a mile of that gate, you'll never see your man again. Understood?"

"Yes, I understand."

"Good."

Click.

Chapter 32

It was a strange day, to say the least, with Matt and Chris "forced" to fish, in order to preserve the false narrative of their being guests at Ralph's ranch exclusively for the purpose of fly fishing. That's not to say that the two didn't enjoy catching one large brown trout after another as they drifted down the beautiful waters of the Beaverhead. Often, both men would have fish on their lines at the same time. Under any other circumstances, they would have been elated.

But the mood aboard the boat this day was somber. Ralph deftly guided the drift boat past boulders and around other boats anchored at various points along the river, often without uttering a single word for as much as twenty minutes or more at a time. His silence allowed Matt and Chris to discuss Clint and Shorty's predicament freely without being interrupted. Occasionally, they needed to stop talking, but only when they approached other boats on the river, or when they drifted past a bridge with other anglers present. The six-hour day felt as though it would never end.

But end it did.

By the time they reached the takeout point at Barrett's Diversion, Matt and Chris couldn't wait to get out of the boat.

As soon as they reached the ranch, Matt hurried into the kitchen and called Clint.

"Have you heard anything more?" he inquired.

"I got a phone call just past four."

"What'd they say?"

"They weren't too happy about the five thousand dollars. But, you and Ralph were right about one thing. I think it bought us a little time. Someone is going to drop off an envelope around midnight with some kind of proof that Shorty's still alive."

"What kind of proof?"

"He didn't say."

"Probably be some kind of picture of Shorty with a newspaper or something else in the picture with the date showing. That's usually how it goes with these things," Matt advised Clint. "Did you get any kind of feel for who they might be?"

"Actually, yes," Clint replied.

"Oh, *really*?"

"He referred to my being a white man several times. There's no doubt in my mind that we're talking about Indians here. I'm *convinced* of it."

"Have you had any kind of trouble lately with any Indians?"

"Not really. But you know how people are. It could be anybody—and for any reason."

"Well, at least we have *some* kind of direction," Matt offered. "We're heading out of here in a little while to check out as many bars as we can in the area. Hopefully, we'll get lucky and run into a bunch of Indians with big mouths."

"I hope so. Because sooner or later this bunch is going to get tired of waiting for their money. That's when things could get really ugly."

"Maybe so," agreed Matt, "but right now, I'd say we're okay for a while at least. So hang in there — and don't give up hope."

Matt hung up the phone.

Man, am I full of shit, or what?

Chris was in the living room watching TV.

"Are you ready to go?" Matt asked. "We've got a lot to do tonight. And the sooner we get started, the better."

"I'm ready when you are."

"Let's go then."

The first place they stopped was the Panther's Den, on State Highway 91 South, just north of the Pizza Hut. It was a tiny watering hole, not more than forty feet deep and about fifteen feet wide, married to a pawnshop of similar dimensions. There was a narrow hallway separating the two establishments that led to an upstairs apartment. Each business had an identical neon sign in its window — the only difference between them being the messages they conveyed. Matt had no doubt they were sold to the respective owners at a "special" discount.

The gravel parking lot adjacent to the bar held a half dozen pickups, each in worse condition than the other. It reminded Matt of so many similar places back home in the Catskills. Depressed areas had much in common, regardless of where in the country they were located. Luckily, Roscoe, owing to the attraction of its nearby blue-ribbon trout streams, remained somewhat above the financial waterline of the surrounding towns in the area.

The front door was slightly ajar, and once the two men entered, it became apparent to Matt why: smoke—lots of it. Apparently, this part of the country hadn't gotten the memo regarding the dangers of tobacco products. The blue haze that hung over the heads of the patrons was so thick it could have floated a boat.

There was an ancient wooden bar on the left that ran almost the entire length of the room. The opposite wall was lined with half-a-dozen-or-so, round, wooden tables. A small pool table, with a green-shaded light above it, sat in the rear, in front of a wall with two doors: one marked "His and Hers"; and another with "Private" on it. Judging by the absence of females, Matt figured that the "Hers" part of the bathroom sign was just a formality. This place was only for serious drinkers and shooting pool, *not* for socializing with members of the opposite sex.

Matt scanned the faces of the patrons and quickly concluded that there were no Native Americans present. He and Chris were just about to leave when the bartender, a gray-haired man in his late sixties with a prosthetic left arm, leaned across the bar. *Semper fi* was tattooed on his good limb.

"What'll ya have, guys?"

"Actually, we were just leaving," Matt replied. Then, he paused. He had an idea. "On second thought, I'll have a Coke . . . oh, what the hell . . . make it a beer. What've you got on tap?"

"Coors and Bud."

"Well, since I hate Bud, better make it a Coors. In fact, make it *two* — one for me and one for my friend."

As the bartender poured the beers, Chris gave Matt a sideways glance as if to say *What the hell is* this *all about?*

Matt winked. "Have a seat. I'm buying."

Always quick on the uptake, Chris nodded and sat down on a stool alongside Matt. "This better be good," he laughed.

"Relax. You'll see."

The bartender had returned with the beers, and he placed cardboard coasters in front of the men, setting a frosty mug of beer on each. "That'll be five dollars."

Chris sat stone-faced, while Matt fished his wallet out of his back pocket and handed the man a twenty. "Keep the change."

The bartender picked up the bill with the prosthesis and held it up for inspection. "Usually when somebody tips like that," he said, "they're looking for something in return. I'll be right back . . . with your change."

Matt reached out and put his hand on the bartender's good arm. "No need. I'm just looking for a little information, that's all. Got a minute?"

"What're you, a cop?"

Matt dodged. "Not really. We're just looking for a couple of fellows — Indians actually. I wondered if you can tell me where that kind might hang out?"

"Well we don't allow *that kind* in here, that's for sure."

"I kind of noticed." Matt took a long draught of his beer.

"There's only one place around here where they serve Indians," the bartender informed Matt. "And they don't serve whites — *just* Indians."

"And that would be?"

"Halfway between here and Twin Bridges. Just head back out on Ninety One, then pick up Forty One on your right. Johnny's is just past Turtle Road on the left."

"How far is that?" Chris asked.

"Oh, probably about twenty miles," the bartender informed him. "So, uh, what do you want with these Indians — if you don't mind me asking?"

Matt downed the remainder of his beer without answering. "Thanks for your help."

It was about a forty-five minute drive to Johnny's, and along the way, Chris bombarded Matt with questions. Mostly, he wanted to know why they weren't checking out the other dozen or so bars in Dillon.

"You heard the man," Matt said. "Johnny's is the only place around that serves Indians. In case you've forgotten, we don't have a hell of a lot of time."

Chris processed that response and had another question: "I take it you're convinced that it's definitely Indians that took Shorty."

"No. Not completely. But based on what Clint said, it's a pretty good bet. I'd rather we concentrate on that angle for now, and maybe save some time."

Chris's silence was all the affirmation Matt needed.

Johnny's didn't *have* a neon sign. It was lucky it had a sign at all. Had it not been for the street lamp perched precariously above what appeared to be a doublewide trailer, they might have missed it. The sign, if one could call it that, was the word "Johnny's" spelled out with individual, stick-on, reflective letters affixed to a white mailbox on a wrought iron post. It was situated at one end of the dirt parking area.

Two pickups and an ancient Volkswagen Beetle were cozied up to the solid wood, front door. There *was* a neon sign in one of the windows, but it barely functioned. It blinked and sputtered, misspelling "Coors Lite" with one of the O's and the letter E missing.

"Not very inviting," whispered Chris, as the pair made their way from the rental vehicle, which Matt had parked across the street on the shoulder of the two-lane road.

"Oh, I don't know," Matt said. "It's got a certain flair to it. Reminds me of a strip joint over on the other side of Monticello. I think *that* was called Johnny's, too, come to think of it." The images of sweaty females, barely of legal age, writhing half naked under hot spotlights came to mind.

Chris laughed. "Never had the pleasure."

"You didn't miss a thing," Matt assured him. "I guarantee it."

"I'll have to take your word for it."

Matt took a deep breath as they approached the door. "Ready?"

"Yeah, what the hell, let's do it!"

Chapter 33

At the exact moment that Bobcat was chatting with the clerk at the Sunoco service station in Walton, Al Coif was pulling the little blue Datsun onto the grassy shoulder of the road in front of the barn on DuCoff Road, just off State Highway 206.

He had spotted this particular barn several weeks ago, and now he couldn't wait to see it burn. He turned off the ignition and sat back in the seat, letting the darkness of the night envelope him. He removed the ever-present Zippo lighter from his pocket, and began opening and closing the lid, which made a crisp, metallic *snap* each time it closed. The sound was as soothing to him as a mother's heartbeat is to a newborn child.

Al finished his first bottle of beer, and, after a while, opened another, greedily sucking down the contents, and enjoying the feel of the cold liquid sliding down his throat. It was always like this. The first couple of beers tasted great. Then it became more of a ritual, even a chore, as he downed one after another, until, at last, he was able to do what he needed to do.

He got out and staggered back to open the trunk. Seeing the three red, plastic gasoline containers, he felt like a child looking at presents beneath the Christmas tree. His heart began to race, and he could feel the familiar warmth spreading through his body.

It was time.

* * * * *

Bruce Pfeffer was deep asleep within the barn. He'd been more tired than he realized, and so the REM sleep he'd been denied at the campground the night before came easily when given the chance. Before long he was dreaming. At first, his dream was as pleasant as could be.

Then it became a nightmare

* * * * *

One by one, Al removed the three plastic containers of gasoline from the trunk of the Datsun. In his drunken stupor, all he could manage to do was carry one container at a time to the front of the barn. But he finally got all three cans there. He hadn't brought any rags, nor did he have the energy required to scrounge around the exterior of the barn for any kind of kindling. But that didn't matter. He had three cans of gasoline, and that was more than enough to get the barn burning.

Staggering and half falling down, Al splashed the gasoline all around the perimeter of the structure, saturating the dry wood with the volatile liquid. At one point, he stopped to empty his bladder, and nearly fell over while struggling with the zipper on his trousers. He finished relieving himself, and then reached in his pocket for the Zippo. The smooth, cool, reassuring touch of the totem acted much like a prescription sedative, and Al felt any inhibitions he might have had melt away.

He was always reluctant to actually set the fires, and couldn't quite understand the compulsion that drove him to do what he inherently knew was wrong. But driven he was, and he couldn't resist the temptation any longer. He flipped open the lid of the Zippo, and slowly began to make his way around the perimeter of the barn, stopping every few feet to ignite a section of gasoline-soaked wood.

Within minutes, the barn was ablaze. The light from the fire was brighter than any fire Al had ever set before. He stood in front of the doors and watched, hypnotized, as the flames engulfed the structure. Then, gradually, his eyes began to close, and, asleep on his feet, he finally passed out and fell to the ground.

*   *   *   *   *

Bobcat wasn't in any particular hurry to get back to headquarters. His shift would be over in a little more than an hour; by then, the State Police would be patrolling Roscoe until the morning shift took over (in the person of Pete Richards). So he tooled along at the minimum speed limit, content to listen to the occasional crackle from the police radio and watching out for any deer that might be stupid enough to try and cross the highway.

As he topped a rise in the road, something caught his attention off to his left. It was the glow of what appeared to be a bonfire or —

"Holy shit!" he exclaimed. "It's a barn!"

He flipped on his light bar and mashed the Pathfinder's accelerator to the floor, pushing the aging vehicle as hard as he dared toward the fire.

"Ten-Seventy on State Highway Two Oh Six," shouted Bobcat into the mike of the police radio. "Officer needs assistance."

As he approached the intersection of Route 206 and DuCoff Road, he slammed on the brakes and slid the SUV around the corner, then goosed the gas pedal once again and sped to the burning barn.

The first thing Bobcat noticed was a blue Datsun parked on the side of the road. He removed a pen and pad from the pocket of his tunic, quickly copied down the license plate number, and then switched off the engine. Grabbing his Maglite, he jumped out of the Pathfinder, and headed toward the flames. As he approached the barn, he could feel the heat from the fire and smell the fumes from the burning gasoline. Up ahead, he saw something on the ground. It was a body!

Good Christ, I hope I'm not too late.

Bobcat rushed forward to the body, and dropped down on one knee beside what appeared to be a middle-aged man who was unconscious. He grabbed the man's right wrist and felt for a pulse. It was strong and steady. That was a good sign. It was then he noticed the smell of alcohol, and realized that the individual lying on the ground was most likely the perpetrator and that he was probably drunk.

Bobcat felt his face flush with anger, and he slapped the man hard across his cheek. "Wake up!" he shouted. "Is there anybody inside?"

Al Coif blinked a couple of times, and tried to speak, but his words were incoherent.

"Get up, goddamn it!" Bobcat ordered, grabbing Al by his sleeve. He tried to lift him, but couldn't budge the inebriated man. "Answer me. Is there anybody inside that barn?"

Al mumbled something that sounded like "Don't know . . . didn't check."

That was all Bobcat needed to hear. "Stay here!" he ordered. "I'm going in. Don't move!"

He released his grip on Al's shirt and stood up. He rushed to the double doors and, without thinking, grabbed the handle to the one on the right.

"Shit!" he screamed. He yanked his hand back in pain. It burned like hell. "Son of a bitch!"

The handle was red hot. Bobcat looked around for something—anything—that he could use to open the door. Finding nothing, he quickly removed his uniform tie and slipped one end through the loop of the barn door handle and, holding both ends of the material, yanked hard and pulled the door open. The interior was rapidly filling with smoke.

He shone the flashlight's beam quickly around the interior of the barn and, at first, didn't see any sign of life.

Thank God.

Then, just to be sure, he methodically retraced the interior of the burning barn with the flashlight's beam.

Oh, crap!

He detected something in the far left corner.

It's a body!

He hurried forward, smoke filling his lungs, and dropped down alongside what was definitely a man, a *young* man, covered by a tarpaulin. He lifted the tarp, grabbed the man's wrist, and felt for a pulse. It was weak but steady.

He placed his hands under the young man's armpits, and then, using all his strength, he lifted the unconscious body off the floor of the barn and swung it over his shoulder like a sack of potatoes. The effort was so intense that it almost caused Bobcat to lose his balance. He struggled to stay erect, and slowly and deliberately made his way across the dirt floor and out the open door into the night.

Bobcat gulped in huge breaths of fresh air, coughing as he struggled to clear his lungs of the acrid smoke. He dropped down to his knees and deposited the unconscious youth onto the ground, then checked for a pulse.

It was faint and barely perceptible.

"Damn," he said aloud. "Come on, pal, don't die on me!"

He cleared the victim's mouth, and immediately began administering CPR. After about five minutes, which seemed to last an eternity, he was rewarded for his efforts when the young man coughed once, twice, and then vomited into the air, narrowly missing Bobcat's face.

"It's okay, buddy," he reassured the youth. "You're going to be okay. Just breathe."

When he was confident that the young man was going to keep breathing, Bobcat spun around and looked for the arsonist.

He was gone. And so was the blue Datsun.

Chapter 34

Montana

Walter took the picture he'd taken of Shorty back to his trailer. He placed it in a manila envelope, then grabbed a sheet of paper and hastily scribbled a note that read: *"Here's your proof! If we don't get some more money soon it won't be so pretty next time."*

He placed the note in the envelope, licked the flap, and sealed it. A glance at the clock on the kitchen wall informed him that the time was just past nine. He planned to drop off the envelope around eleven, which left him with a couple of hours to kill. He set the timer on the microwave to go off in ninety minutes, then walked into the living room and plopped down on the couch. He switched on the TV set with the remote control, and scrolled through the channels until he came to an episode of *Cops*. Within a matter of minutes he was fully absorbed in the program.

It took just longer than that to fall asleep.

When the microwave timer beeped exactly ninety minutes later, Walter instinctively jumped to his feet and started for the kitchen. His mind was still foggy from the effects of sleep, and it took a moment before he could focus. The kitchen clock read eleven-fourteen.

Oh shit!

Walter grabbed the manila envelope off of the kitchen table and headed out the door of the trailer. The night air was cool, which helped clear his head. He fired up the Ford pickup, threw it into gear, then tromped down on the gas pedal, and headed in the direction of Clint Davidson's ranch.

Ten minutes later, he arrived at the spot where he and Jimmy had last parked. He sprinted quietly from the truck to the ranch gates, and placed the envelope next to them on the ground.

In less than a half hour, he was back at the trailer.

*   *   *   *   *

Clint decided to ride his favorite horse, Dusty, out to the gate to retrieve the promised proof of Shorty's well-being. He figured that if the kidnappers were watching, they would feel less threatened at seeing a horse rather than a vehicle approaching the drop-off location.

He quickly saddled the chestnut mare, climbed aboard, and gently nudged her sides with the heels of his boots, saying, "Giddy up, girl!"

It was an easy mile or so to the entrance to the ranch, and horse and rider covered the distance in less than ten minutes. Clint tethered the mare to a fence post and climbed down. He pulled a mini flashlight from his pocket and shone the beam around the base of the double gates. He immediately spotted a large white envelope wedged firmly between the two of them.

Clint looked around for any sign of the kidnappers, and when he was confident that no one was watching, used his pocketknife to open the envelope.

"Well I'll be . . . " he whispered.

There, in glorious living color, was a picture of Shorty McMahon. And in his lap was a copy of the *Montana Standard* with that day's date on it, just as Matt had predicted.

Thank God.

Clint mounted Dusty and headed back to the ranch. As he rode, he thought about Shorty.

Okay, my friend. I know you're alive, but what do I do now?

*   *   *   *   *

The interior of Johnny's was not at all what Matt had expected. There was a bar, of course, but there were no strippers. Fair enough. In fact, there was only one female in the place, and she was the bartender. There were two other individuals present, both elderly Native American men who were situated all the way down at the right-hand end of the bar, each with a mug of beer in front of him.

The first thing Matt noticed was how quiet it was. The only noise came from the huge flat screen TV mounted on the wall. It was tuned to CNN, and the volume was turned down low. Anderson Cooper's distinctive face, topped by his signature white hair, filled the center of the screen. He was speaking with a Democratic Party operative about the unlikely results of the presidential election.

"Christ, if I wanted to see *that* asshole, I could have stayed at home," whispered Chris.

Matt's attention, however, wasn't focused upon the television. He was looking at the bartender. She was a college-aged Native American with long black hair, worn in perfectly plaited braids that hung down almost to her breasts. The expression she wore said more than any words she could speak. It was obvious they were not welcome there.

"Evening," Matt said. "I hope there isn't a problem."

"No *problem*, white man," said the young woman. "No *service*, either. The only problem will be if you and your friend don't turn around and leave."

Matt smiled. He'd been in this same situation many times before, most recently when he had entered a topless bar, looking for the killer of a known meth dealer back in the Roscoe area.

He held up his hand in the traditional "peace" sign.

"We're not looking for any trouble. Actually, I'm hoping we might be able to help each other."

"Really," said the girl.

"That's right."

"Well I can't imagine anything you could do to help *me*, so what is it that you think I could do to help *you*?"

"We're looking for any of your people who might be flashing a lot of money. You know, like maybe they won the lottery or something."

"You mean *Indians*," she said, her voice flat in its tone.

"Well, I wasn't sure how to phrase it," replied Matt. "But since you said it, okay, yes."

"What do you want with them?"

"That's not something I can discuss."

The young woman reflected for a moment on what Matt had just said. "And what was it exactly that you were going to help *me* with?" she asked.

Matt looked down toward the two men at the end of the bar. "I can help you by not asking *them* for their identification, or bothering to run that information for any outstanding warrants." Matt flashed his Roscoe police badge slowly enough for the girl to see it, but fast enough to prevent her from actually reading what it said.

The girl frowned. "Hey," she said. "I've got one just like that. I bought *mine* online from a police surplus site. Where'd you get *yours*?"

Ignoring the sarcasm, Matt continued, "So, where were we? Oh, I remember. You were wracking your brain to think of whether or not anybody has been in lately with a lot of cash."

Another frown.

"*Can't* remember? Or *won't*?"

A smile.

"Okay," Matt said. "Let's not waste each other's time. If you must know, we're investigating a phony insurance claim. Can you help us or not?"

Another smile.

"What's so funny?" Matt asked.

Chris had started to walk slowly down toward the end of the bar where the only other two patrons were located.

"Hang on a second," Matt advised Chris. "I think our friendly bartender may have something to tell us that you might want to hear."

Chris stopped, turned around, and rejoined his partner.

"Look," the girl began, "I don't want any trouble. I haven't seen anyone with a lot of money, and I don't know anything about any insurance claim. I *do* know that every time something happens around here, *we're* always the first ones to get blamed."

"Nobody said anything about blame. We're just trying to find these fellows before they spend all the money and get themselves into more trouble than they're already in. I wouldn't care if it turned out to be Barack Obama who filed a phony claim. Whoever's responsible is going down, whether they're Indians *or* white men, it makes no difference to me."

Matt took out one of the bogus business cards he carried with him, just for times like this, and placed it on the bar in front of the young woman. It had his name on it and the logo of a prominent insurance company. His title was listed as Claims Investigator.

"I'd really appreciate it if you keep this to yourself, and if you hear anything, anything at all that you think might help . . . well, I'd appreciate it if you'd give me a call."

"Is that a cell?" asked the girl, pointing to the phone clipped to Matt's belt.

"Yeah, why?"

"Cell service sucks around here."

Matt smiled. "You got *that* right," he agreed. "We're staying at the Big Sky Fin and Fur Resort, and they have a land line. If you can't get through to me on the cell, leave a message there and I'll get in touch."

Chris smiled at the two men at the end of the bar.

"Let's go," Matt said. "Thank you for your time, young lady. Oh, by the way, what's your name . . . uh . . . just in case you decide to call?"

"Pocahontas."

Matt waved a hand dismissively in the air. "Whatever."

It was well past one in the morning by the time Matt and Chris arrived back at the resort. To their surprise, Ralph was waiting for them in the kitchen.

"Well, you were right, Matt" he said. "Clint called me just past midnight. Shorty's alive. And just like you said they would, they took a picture of him holding a copy of today's *Standard*." Then, in an obvious reference to Robert DeNiro's character in the film *Analyze This*, he pointed his middle and index fingers in Matt's direction and said, "You . . . you're very good . . . you."

Matt smiled and was quiet for a moment.

"Anything wrong?" Ralph asked.

"No, no, I'm just thinking about what to do next."

"How'd you two make out in town? Any progress?"

"Nah, well, maybe," Chris answered. "We ended up at a place called Johnny's. Ever hear of it?"

"Sure," replied Ralph. "It's an Indian hangout. Nobody else would be caught dead in there. So I take it you definitely think it's Indians that done this, huh?"

"No," Matt answered. "But it's all we've got right now, so we're working it hard."

Ralph looked at Chris for support.

Chris shrugged his shoulders.

"Well, I don't know about you fellers, but I think I need to get to bed."

"Sounds like a plan," Matt replied. "Good chance the shit's going to hit the fan tomorrow," he added.

"I can't wait," Chris murmured, as he headed up the stairs toward his room.

Chapter 35

Roscoe, NY

Bobcat could hear sirens in the distance, and as the sound grew closer, a sense of relief flooded over him. While he waited, seated on the ground alongside the young man he had rescued, he gradually became aware of the throbbing pain in his right hand. He looked down and was surprised to see that the entire palm was covered with blisters.

How the hell did that happen?

Then he remembered.

Shit.

He needed to get medical attention soon. He looked down at the young man lying on the ground beside him. "Hey," he whispered, "are you doing okay?"

The youth opened his eyes and tried to speak, but was immediately engulfed in a coughing fit. Finally, when he had regained his breath, he tried again. "What happened?" he whispered, his voice ragged from the effects of the smoke.

"Some jackass set the barn on fire. It's a good thing I was passing by, or you'd be a goner."

The young man closed his eyes, then opened them again. "I'm not in any trouble, am I?" he asked. "I mean, I didn't have anything to do with—"

"Relax, just relax. You're definitely not in any kind of trouble," Bobcat assured him. "Do you think you can stand?"

The young man sat up, then tried standing. He immediately lost his balance and fell back onto the ground.

"Hey, hey, take it easy," Bobcat advised. Without thinking, he extended his right hand toward the young student's. "Here, let me help you up."

As soon as his hand made contact with the young man's hand, Bobcat realized his mistake. But it was too late. He gritted his teeth against the pain, and pulled the boy to a standing position. In an effort to not scream, he emitted a low, guttural sound akin to that of a wild animal.

The college student immediately pulled his hand away. "Sorry," he apologized. "What happened to your hand?"

Bobcat ignored the question.

Just then, several police cars, a fire truck, and an EMS vehicle pulled up to the property. By now, the barn was completely engulfed in flames.

"I don't think there's any rush," Bobcat advised the first firefighter he saw. "Might as well let it burn."

"Is this the guy who set the fire?" asked a State policeman.

Bobcat shook his head and laughed. "No, no. He was just sleeping in the barn. The guy who set the fire took off. I got his license plate, though, so we ought to be able to find him easy enough."

He pulled the pad out of his tunic pocket and waited as the State trooper copied the information onto a pad of his own.

"Why don't you let me take care of rounding up the perp," Bobcat suggested. "I'd really like to be the one to take him down—that is, *if* you wouldn't mind."

The State trooper smiled. "Be my guest," he suggested. "We're a little shorthanded right now, anyway, so that would be a big help. But first, you might want to get that hand attended to."

Bobcat grimaced and looked down at his hand. "I guess you're right."

"I'd definitely get somebody from EMS to take a look at it," the trooper said. Then, turning toward the boy, he asked, "And how's this young man doing?"

"Oh, I'm okay," answered the student. "I should probably be getting on my way." Buoyed by a sense of relief, he looked at the two men and asked, "Any chance of getting a lift into Roscoe?"

"I'll give you a ride," Bobcat offered. "Just let me get this hand looked at first."

"Sure. No problem."

"And while we're at it, you ought to let them have a look-see at you, too."

The two men started walking toward the EMS truck.

Ten minutes later, his hand swathed with antiseptic and wrapped in gauze, Bobcat motioned the student toward the Pathfinder. "Let's go, pal. I'll run you into town."

The ride to Roscoe took fifteen minutes.

All the while, Bobcat was fixated on the thought of apprehending the arsonist.

By the time he dropped off the young man at the Roscoe Diner, he had come to the realization that finding the firebug could wait until morning. He needed sleep, and he needed it badly.

*   *   *   *   *

When he'd been awakened by Bobcat, Al's immediate reaction was to play dead, which wasn't that difficult considering all the beer he'd consumed. When the patrolman had left him unattended, he knew his best chance to avoid being arrested was to run, and that's exactly what he did.

Al stumbled over the rough ground, away from the burning barn and toward the Datsun. The flickering light from the fire behind him cast irregular shadows over the landscape, making it that much more difficult to navigate. Twice he tumbled to the ground, once hard enough to open a cut over his left eye. With blood dripping down his cheek, Al managed to get to the car, open the door, and climb inside.

He fumbled in his pants pocket for the keys, extracted them, and promptly dropped them onto the floorboard. "Shit," he muttered. "Where the hell did you go?" He felt around the floor of the cab, but couldn't find the keys. Between the blood flowing over his left eye and the hazy fog of his inebriation, he could barely see. Finally, his fingers closed on the key ring. He raised his hand in triumph and banged his head on the underside of the steering wheel. "Son of a bitch!" he shouted.

Al inserted the key into the ignition, depressed the clutch pedal, and started the engine. He never used the hand brake, choosing instead to leave the transmission in first gear, so all he had to do was slowly release the clutch while feathering the gas pedal, and he'd be on his way. But that was when he was sober. Now, it took three tries before he was able to get the little car moving without stalling. "Third time's a charm," he slurred, immensely pleased with his success.

"Why the hell can't I see," he murmured. "Oh yeah, it helps if you've got the lights on, dummy," he admonished himself. He giggled and reached for the light switch. The sudden illumination sent a wave of pain through his alcohol-riddled brain, and he squinted against the bright light of the dashboard. The driver side window was open, and the cool night air swirled around his head as the vehicle picked up speed as it headed down the road.

The road itself was barely visible, so Al made a concerted effort to follow the painted center line as closely as he could, holding the steering wheel in a death grip, as the Datsun veered left and right along the macadam highway. *Maybe I can make it after all*, he thought, and his progress was fairly impressive—that is until the deer darted out into the center of the road.

"Oh, fuck!" yelled Al, as he yanked the steering wheel hard to the right in a futile attempt to avoid the animal. But he was on a curving section of the road alongside the Pepacton Reservoir, and the sudden shift in the car's direction, coupled with the radical change in its center of gravity, sent the little Datsun careening off the road, over the soft shoulder, and down a steep embankment toward the reservoir below. Al frantically pressed with all his might on the brake pedal, but his efforts had no effect at all.

Suddenly, he felt the car starting to list to his right, and the steering wheel was wrenched violently from his hands, as the car began to tumble toward the water. Over and over it went, until suddenly it slammed into something hard and everything went black.

The large evergreen tree that had halted the Datsun's travel and kept it from plunging into the water, had also crushed the passenger side door, effectively trapping Al inside, with only the driver side door available as an exit. The sudden impact had caused Al's head to make contact with the doorpost, knocking him unconscious. Now, as he struggled to regain control of his faculties, he realized that getting out was not going to be an easy task.

The Datsun's left side tires were off the ground, and the car was resting against the tree at better than a forty-five degree angle. But the main problem was that the driver's side door was now in nearly the position where the roof normally would be—*above* him. He strained with all his might to reach the door handle, and let out a sigh of relief when he finally did. But of course he couldn't open the door, because its entire weight was pressing down from above, owing to its extreme juxtaposition. He tried several more times, but his efforts were in vain.

The last attempt brought on a wave of nausea so intense that it quickly overcame him, and he promptly vomited and passed out. He awoke briefly a few minutes later, noted how bright the stars appeared in the dark sky, and made a decision to go back to sleep.

Chapter 36

Montana

Ronald White Feather was beginning to become concerned. The whole kidnapping idea had never particularly appealed to him, and his deep, abiding sensibilities for the animal kingdom had been seriously offended when they had murdered the prize bull.

Now, as he sat quietly in the living room of the modular home, he examined his predicament even more closely. Ronald didn't know much about the law, but he remembered reading somewhere that a conviction for kidnapping carried with it the death penalty. He also had read that a victim had to be taken across state lines for that to be in effect. (Actually, he was confusing kidnapping with the Mann Act, which was signed into law by President Taft in 1910, and made it a crime to transport women across state lines "for the purpose of prostitution or debauchery, or for any other immoral purpose.")

No matter what the potential punishment, Ronald, at age 25, could foresee only a bad ending in his future. In order to minimize the impact of the kidnapping, he needed to separate himself from his confederates at the earliest possible opportunity. But he needed a plan. And right now he had none.

*   *   *   *   *

Jimmy Blackwater and Henry Golden Eagle were glad to be out of house. As they drove through the dark toward Johnny's, the two discussed the latest news regarding the ransom money.

"You know, Henry," Jimmy said, "we're taking a really big chance for not very much money. I mean, what are we talking about here, a couple of thousand dollars apiece?"

Henry concentrated on the road. Jimmy was always bitching and moaning about something, he thought. He was a Crow, which loosely translated meant "people who lived in earthen lodges." He had no vision—just like his people, who came from somewhere near the headwaters of the Mississippi, and then settled in the Dakotas. Only a foolish people would leave a fertile land for one as desolate as the Badlands. *Jimmy's just a fool. Let him talk.*

Jimmy continued talking, as if on cue. "What if they never give us all the money? Then what? I don't like it."

"Why don't you just shut up," Henry barked. "Walter knows what he's doing. Nobody has any idea how much money that old rancher, Davidson, *really* has. This is just the beginning. You'll see."

"Well, I hope you're right. That foreman seems to be a nice guy, and I, for one, don't want to see anything happen to him."

"Nothing's going to *happen* to him," Henry insisted. "We gave our word. We all did. After all, we're not murderers."

"Yeah, but I'm not so sure about Walter," Jimmy replied. "I mean, think about it. Once we have the money, do you *really* think that old man's going to be willing to just let Shorty go?"

"Why not?"

"Because . . . because . . . oh . . . never mind."

"Because *what*?" shouted Henry.

"Because, for one thing, Shorty knows our voices. And who knows what *else* he knows. Hell, he's smart. He's probably figured out a lot more than he lets on."

Henry steered the pickup off the road and onto the dirt parking area alongside Johnny's. "That's enough, Jimmy. Let's just get high. Forget all about this whole thing for a while. Okay? Deal?" He stuck out his hand, palm side up.

Jimmy made a pouting face like a small boy might, then slapped Henry's open hand—hard. "Deal," he agreed. "But let's just keep our options open, okay?"

"Whatever," muttered Henry. "Hey, I think *Ehawee* is working tonight. There's her car." He pointed to a battered VW Bug, painted bright pink, with flowered decals on it. "See?"

Jimmy smiled.

"See," said Henry. "What'd I tell you? it's all good. Princess Laughing Maid is in the house."

"Fuck you, Flathead," laughed Jimmy.

"Eat me, Crow!"

*   *   *   *   *

Shorty sat in the dark, the little transistor radio playing softly beside him on the bed. All his senses told him that time was running out. It didn't take a genius to know that once the "Four Little Injuns," as he liked to refer to his captors, had gotten what they wanted, his days were numbered. He needed to escape. But *how*?

His best chance was when he was being guarded by only one of the Indians, and the others were out of the house. Like tonight, for instance.

Relax. Don't do anything hasty.

But time was running out.

"Hey!" shouted Shorty. "I need to go to the john."

Shorty knew that Injun Four was probably asleep, and he'd heard Injun One and Injun Two talking earlier about going out drinking, so that left Injun Three as this evening's "guard du jour."

"Hey, how about it, Injun Three? I've gotta go Number Two. If somebody doesn't let me in the john soon, it's gonna get messy."

Shorty laughed quietly to himself. If it weren't for his sense of humor, he might never have survived as long as he had. Gallows humor was his specialty.

"How about it?" he repeated. "Anybody home?"

Shorty heard a scuffling sound in the living room.

"Relax, white man. Hold your horses. I'm coming."

And I'm going, thought Shorty. "If you don't get here soon, I'm gonna shit my pants."

A minute or so later, there were footsteps outside the bedroom door, then a key was inserted in the lock, and the door was pulled open.

"On your feet, white man," Ronald White Feather ordered.

Shorty swiveled his legs around until they were draped over the edge of the mattress and touching the floor. Slowly, so as not to lose his balance, he stood up.

"Don't move," commanded Ronald. He bent down and removed the chain attached to Shorty's handcuffs from where it was hooked around the leg of the headboard. Holding the loose end of the chain, he used it to guide his captive out of the bedroom and across the hall to the toilet.

What happened next came as a complete surprise to both of them.

Chapter 37

Roscoe, NY

Bobcat awoke from the dream drenched in perspiration. The details were already a faded memory, but from what he could recall, it had involved being underwater and having his hand caught in a giant clam.

As reality set in, the source of the dream became readily apparent. Bobcat's right hand was on fire. Despite the antiseptic that had been applied the night before, there was no doubt that some kind of infection had set in to the area of his palm that had been burned. And he didn't need a thermometer to know that he was running a fever.

Bobcat picked up the phone next to his bed and punched in the number for police headquarters. Nancy Cooper answered on the second ring.

"Roscoe Police. How may I direct your call?"

"Hi, Nancy. It's Bobcat."

"My, my, what a pleasant surprise."

"I'm sure it is. Is Rick around?"

"He was. Let me check his office and I'll—"

"Never mind," Bobcat said. "I really don't need to speak with him. Just tell him I have to go over to Urgent Care in Livingston Manor. As soon as I get back, I'll run the license plate of that blue Datsun that was at the fire last night."

"What fire?"

"You mean there's something that our intrepid reporter, Nancy Cooper, hasn't heard about yet? Now *there's* a news flash."

"And why do you need to go to Urgent Care?" asked Nancy, ignoring the patrolman's sarcasm.

"I'll tell you when I get back." (Bobcat was enjoying the moment.)

"But—"

"Relax," Bobcat said with a smile in his voice. "I'm just jerking your chain."

"Well that's a relief. So, are you going to tell me or what?"

"What?"

"Bobcat Walker! *What* happened and what's this about a fire?"

"Okay, okay. I'll start at the beginning. I was over in Walton last night, handing out those flyers about the firebug, and when I was headed back over the mountain, I spotted flames over on DuCoff Road. When I got there, there was a barn on fire, and the guy who set the thing was lying on the ground drunk."

"Do you think he's the same guy who's been setting all those other fires?"

"I don't know, but I'd guess he probably is. He drives a blue Datsun, gotta be twenty years old at least, I'd say. Anyway, I got his license plate and I'm going to run it through as soon as—"

"As soon as you get back from Urgent Care. I know. So how come you didn't arrest him on the spot?"

"It's a long story."

"I've got all morning."

"Well, like I said, he was drunk, so I knew he wasn't going anywhere," Bobcat admitted. "When I asked him if there was anybody in the barn, he didn't know, so I had to look inside. I left him there on the ground and when I went to open the barn door, well, the handle was red hot, and that's when I burned my hand."

"How bad is it?"

"Bad enough. I think it's infected, because I know I'm running a fever. That's why I need to get over to Livingston Manor and get it checked out."

The humor had disappeared from Nancy's voice. "Well, you take care . . . and let me know if there's anything you need me to do."

"Well, I could use you to do a little white wash for me, but other than that—"

"Very funny."

"Just don't forget to tell Rick."

"I won't."

* * * * *

Al Coif awoke with a start, and was immediately in a lot of pain. To make matters worse, the interior of the Datsun reeked of stale vomit. At first, he had no idea where he was or how he had gotten there. But slowly, the details of the night before came flooding back into his consciousness. Besides the head wound he had suffered in the collision with the tree, he had several broken ribs and a spiral fracture of his right tibia (probably from pressing so hard on the brake pedal, he thought). He didn't know it, of course, but he was also bleeding internally from a mildly lacerated liver. Under normal circumstances, none of those injuries would have been life threatening, but considering that he was virtually trapped inside an automobile and hidden from the road above, things weren't looking too good.

Al licked his lips, which were as dry as a desert wind, and thought, *Man, what I wouldn't do for a drink of water.* He looked up through the open driver's side window at the sky, and tried to calculate the time based upon the angle of the sun. It must be somewhere between dawn and noon, he reasoned. He reached inside the right pocket of his trousers, and felt around for the Zippo. *Thank God*, he thought, when he located it. The metal of the cigarette lighter felt cool to the touch, and, just knowing that he still had it gave Al a sense of relief.

He closed his eyes and thought briefly of his father, as he invariably did when he had the lighter in his hand.

"What did you do *this* time, Al?" he could hear his father asking him.

"I really screwed up," he whispered in reply. "I screwed up good."

"Well, don't just lie there, boy. Get your ass up and make things right."

Al laughed aloud at the imagined conversation. Oh, how he wished he could do what his father asked. He tried to bring his legs up onto the Datsun's seat, so he could stand on it and reach the door above. But just the barest movement of his right leg resulted in so much pain that it caused him to scream involuntarily.

Oh, God, how am I going to get out of here?

A scuffling sound from the backseat caused him to be silent and just listen. For a minute or so, there was no more noise. Then, it started again.

Scratch! Scratch!

What the hell is that? he thought.

It sounded like a small animal—maybe a squirrel?—trying to dig a hole. Al swiveled his head around and focused his vision on the backseat of the car. Sure enough, there was the source of the sound: a chipmunk, scratching at a cardboard box that had contained a couple of slices of pizza from the previous night's dinner. Just the thought of the food made Al ravenously hungry. He wondered whether or not he had left any uneaten crust inside the box. He reached back, and stretching as best he could, tried to get the fingers of his right hand around a corner of the cardboard container.

The chipmunk chattered angrily at the intrusion into its space, and Al swatted the little rodent away with the back of his hand. At last, he was able to drag the box off the seat and into the front of the car. He opened the carton, but, much to his disappointment, all that it contained were some crumbs and one small piece of crust, which he quickly devoured.

That still left him hungry, and, now, more than ever, thirsty as hell. The act of retrieving the pizza box had also exhausted him. *Imagine that,* he thought, *tired from dragging a cardboard pizza box from the backseat into the front. What a wuss!* He didn't want to think of what kind of shape he must be in for it to have *that* kind of effect on his body.

Al's nose tickled, and he tried to scratch it, and that caused him to sneeze. *Ah-choo!* A lightning bolt of pain seared his chest, as the fractured ribs expanded, then contracted with the effort of the sneeze. Tears welled up in Al's eyes, and he started to weep.

I am so fucked.

Chapter 38

Montana

Matt was certain that the young Indian girl at Johnny's knew something. There had been a glint of recognition that flashed in her eyes the previous night when he'd asked her about seeing any young Indians with a lot of money. Somehow, he needed to find a way to gain her confidence—without spooking her so badly that she'd tip off whoever it was that she was protecting.

He'd never felt so constrained before when working a case. But this was not a typical situation, and that was something he was finally coming to grips with.

"Do you get the same feeling I do about little Miss Pocahontas over at Johnny's?" Matt asked Chris. "I don't think it's my imagination that she knows something."

Chris was sucking the dark chocolate coating off a Milky Way Midnight bar, and, without missing a lick, nodded in agreement, while making an "uh huh" sound.

"Don't let me interrupt your little food frenzy," joked Matt.

The two men were relaxing within the confines of one of Ralph Gilly's drift boats as it made its way down the Beaverhead River with Ralph at the helm. Once again, they had taken to the water in order to maintain the impression of them being just another two clients of the ranch.

However, the charade was beginning to take its toll on the two lawmen, and the frustration at not being much help to their friend's friend was becoming a real burden.

Working together back in New York City, Matt and Chris had always been used to making things happen; they shook the trees and the bad apples fell to the ground. Here, they weren't even permitted the luxury of looking too closely at the fruit, no matter how unsavory it might appear.

"What if we were to really press her?" Chris asked. "You know, threaten her with jail time for withholding information. Some kind of bullshit charge."

"I thought about that," Matt replied. "But she struck me as pretty street smart. I think it'd only make her more determined to keep her mouth shut."

A loud *smack* caught Matt's attention. "Was that a *fish?*"

"I wasn't paying attention," Chris replied.

Matt lifted the tip of the Sage fly rod he was holding and immediately felt it throb. "I think I've got one!" he cried.

"Well it's about time," joked Chris. He'd caught the only fish of the day to that point, a small male brown trout. Matt hadn't had as much as a refusal.

The tension on Matt's end of the rod was immediately transmitted to the fish on the other end of the line, and soon all of the chartreuse floating line had flown through the guides of the rod, with the braided backing following quickly behind it.

"Better set that hook, and set it *hard*," shouted Ralph from the front of the boat. "It's a big rainbow. I saw him take your PMD. Probably a four pounder."

Zzzzzzzzzzz! Matt's borrowed Ross Evolution fly reel was singing loudly in protest, its disc drag doing all it could to slow down the charging trout, which was headed straight for a brush pile on the other side of the river.

"Give him the old down and dirty!" yelled Ralph.

"What's that?"

"Turn the rod sideways, then back the other way. It disorients the fish. Confuses 'em."

Matt did as he was instructed, and gradually the large trout slowed its charge for the other side of the river.

After a half dozen acrobatic leaps, the fish began to tire, and five minutes later, Matt had retrieved all the backing and most of the floating line onto the reel. Soon, the fish's silvery sides broke the surface of the water as it lay spent, waiting only to be netted and released. A bright magenta slash colored its side.

"Here," offered Chris. "Let me land him for you." He leaned over the side of the boat and grasped the braided leader in his right hand, reaching for the tippet section with his left. As he pulled the exhausted hen fish toward the side of the boat, she gave one last kick with her tail and the tippet snapped with a loud *pop!* Chris looked back at Matt and smiled. "Oops."

"Yeah, oops to you, too," Matt laughed.

"You mean you're not mad?"

"Nope," Matt replied. "Actually I'm relieved. Hey, Ralph! Let's get this thing back to dry land. No offense, buddy, but I've had all the fishing I can handle."

Chris laughed. "I think I know *exactly* how you feel. I was wondering when you'd get tired of pretending. This fake fishing shit is getting on my nerves."

"I don't really know what we can do about finding these goddamn kidnappers," Matt confided. "But this doing nothing just isn't working."

Ralph leaned on the oars, and kept doing so until they had finished their drift and reached the take-out.

"Sorry, Ralph," Matt said. "But I just don't feel right fishing all day while Shorty's still missing. We came here to help, not to fish."

"Hey, man," replied Ralph. "No apologies necessary. I just wish I could be of more help myself."

Matt looked at Ralph and smiled. "You're doing plenty," he assured him. "It's *us* who need to do more."

* * * * *

Without warning, all the lights had gone out in the double wide. Although Shorty couldn't see through the blindfold, he was able to discern light and dark. Now, it was *really* dark.

"Shit!" exclaimed Ronald. "Don't move!"

Besides realizing that something had happened, Shorty also detected a note of panic in his captor's voice. He didn't know exactly what had happened to make the lights go out, but he knew an opportunity when it presented itself — and this was it.

Without hesitating, he reached out for the chain that Ronald was holding. Grasping it firmly in both hands, he jerked as hard as he could.

"Hey!" Ronald yelled in surprise. "What are you doing?"

The chain came free from Ronald's hands, and Shorty staggered forward until he made contact with the young Indian's back. Estimating where he thought the man's head ought to be, he lifted his arms high into the air and then brought them down hard. *Thunk!* He hit Ronald right on top of his head, knocking him to the ground. Shorty dropped to the floor and, using all his strength, he spread his arms as far apart as he could, forced them over Ronald's head, and closed them around his neck. Then he squeezed — hard! Ronald struggled to free himself from the older man's grip, but it was no use. He was no match for the practiced strength of the hired hand.

Shorty continued to squeeze until Ronald lost consciousness. His intention was not to kill him, but to be absolutely sure he was incapacitated. When he was certain that Ronald wasn't going to resist, he forced his handcuffed hands into each of Ronald's pockets until he found a key ring full of keys.

"You damn sure better have a key to these handcuffs," whispered Shorty into the unconscious man's ear, "or I'm gonna have one hell of a time getting them off."

After trying several of the keys on the key ring, Shorty finally found the one he was after. In less than a minute his hands were free, and he immediately removed the blindfold from his eyes. In another minute, the handcuffs were around Ronald's wrists. Shorty undid the cuffs from around his ankles and breathed a sigh of relief. Then, he placed them around Ronald's ankles, saying, "Turn about is fair play . . . I guess." He shoved the key ring in his pocket.

The double wide's interior was pitch black at first, but gradually the moonlight filtering in through the windows allowed Shorty to get his bearings.

Leaving Ronald on the floor outside the bathroom, he made his way toward the living room area.

Jesus. What a dump. Snack food wrappers and empty beer cans littered the interior of the trailer. It was anybody's guess how long the power would be off, so had to move as quickly as he could. He also wanted to get as far away from there as possible, because if he didn't, there was no telling what they would do to him.

* * * * *

Janice Trueblood had worked as a barmaid at Johnny's for nearly a decade, but her youthful looks still drew inquisitive stares from newcomers to the establishment, who wondered if she were even of legal age. However, her no-nonsense demeanor quickly served notice to anyone who might dismiss her as a lightweight, and left little doubt as to who was in charge. As an added reminder, a fully loaded 12-gauge, Remington pump-action shotgun sat nearby the register, just in case.

Those who knew her well called her by her Lakota Sioux middle name of *Ehawee*, which meant Laughing Maid. Everyone else just called her Janice.

Jimmy Blackwater pushed through the front entrance to Johnny's, and sauntered inside, followed closely behind by Henry Golden Eagle. Their appearance brought a smile to Janice's face.

"Well, well," she said. "Look what the cat dragged in."

"*Hola, Ehawee*," Jimmy said with a smile. Mixing Spanish with his Native American language was something he enjoyed doing. It confused a lot of people, which made him feel just the tiniest bit superior. But to those who knew him, it had become mostly passé, even a bit annoying.

"Hi, Janice," said Henry, deliberately eschewing the linguistic gymnastics practiced by his friend. "How about a couple of Coors?" He pulled out one of his crisp new fifty dollar bills and laid it on the bar top.

"Coming right up," replied Janice, picking up the bill and holding it up to the ceiling light for a prolonged inspection. "Ink dry yet?" she inquired with a broad smile.

"Ha, ha. Very funny. Why would you say a thing like that?" Henry asked.

"Oh, I don't know. I guess because I've never seen you in here with anything besides a bunch of singles in your wallet."

"Well, it just so happens that things have been going very well for us lately. Isn't that right, Jimmy?" He turned to his friend for support, but Jimmy wasn't listening. His attention was focused on the flat screen TV behind the bar, which was showing a music video featuring a scantily clad young woman dancing to some outdated rock music.

"I think Jimmy is a little preoccupied," laughed Janice.

Henry shrugged his shoulders. "Yeah, well, you know Jimmy. He's just a horny toad in heat."

"So, Henry, what *have* you guys been up to, anyway?"

"Oh, same old, same old."

Janice raised an eyebrow. "Really?"

"Yeah. Why?"

"Oh, nothing," she replied with a laugh. "I just thought you might have robbed a bank or something."

Henry squinted at the young girl. "What's *that* supposed to mean?"

Janice placed both hands on her hips. "Look, it's pretty obvious that you two have come into some money. I mean, since when are you waving fifty-dollar bills around like a fly swatter?" She hesitated before adding, "I guess that's why those two men were around earlier, looking for—"

"What two men?"

Janice shrugged her shoulders and rolled her eyes.

Henry leaned across the bar. "*What* two men?" he repeated, this time more quietly. "And what was it they were looking for?"

Jimmy had grown weary of the music video, and slid closer to Henry, scooping up one of the mugs of beer that Janice had placed on the bar top next to the change from Henry's fifty-dollar bill. "What's going on?" he inquired.

"That's what I'm trying to find out from little Princess Laughing Maid," Henry replied, his voice dripping with sarcasm. "How about it, *Ehawee*?"

Janice leaned in close to the two men. "Okay, well, these two *palefaces* came in tonight looking for any, quote, unquote, Indians who might be showing off a lot of cash. At first, they tried to make me think they were cops, and the one guy even flashed some kind of badge. I didn't get a close look at it, but I'm pretty sure it was bogus."

"Any idea what they wanted?" Henry asked.

"Yeah. Something about a phony insurance claim—"

Jimmy looked at Henry and pantomimed, "See? I told you."

"You told me *what*?"

"I told you this whole thing was a bad idea."

"Maybe it's just a coincidence," Henry posited.

Janice tapped Henry on the shoulder. "Here. See. He gave me this card." She held out the card she'd been given.

Henry yanked the card from Janice's hand and examined it closely. "Who the hell is Matt Davis? And where the heck is area code 607?"

"Your guess is as good as mine," Janice said. "Google it. One thing's for sure, they weren't from around here."

"How long ago were they here?" Jimmy asked.

"Oh, maybe two hours ago. Three, tops."

Henry picked up his change, leaving a five-dollar bill for Janice, then grabbed his friend's arm, pulling him away from the bar. "Come on, Jimmy. We've gotta warn the others—just in case. Thanks, *Ehawee*."

Janice lifted up the hinged section of the counter and slipped out from behind the bar. "Where are you going?" she asked. "Are you guys in trouble? Maybe I can help. What do those guys want with you?"

"Take it easy, *Ehawee*," Jimmy whispered. "The less you know, the better. Trust me. Just don't tell anyone we were here tonight, okay?"

Janice nodded. "I promise. Not a word."

"Good," said Henry. "Now get back behind that bar and wave good night, just like you always do."

Janice lifted up the hinged section of the counter and dipped back under to the other side, closing it behind her. "Night, boys!" she called. "See you again."

But Henry and Jimmy were already out the door.

"Men," said Janice, with an exaggerated toss of her head. "Can't live with 'em . . . and I don't really *want* to."

Two older men down at the far end of the bar laughed, and Janice laughed in response. But what she was thinking wasn't funny at all.

Chapter 39

Roscoe, NY

The sun was high in the sky, and Al Coif was really starting to feel the effects of his injuries. The midday heat wasn't helping any, but, at least the driver's side window was open, so he wasn't in any danger of suffocating. However, he *was* dehydrated from all the beer he had drunk the previous evening, and he knew he wouldn't last long if he didn't get some water to drink soon. But first he had to find a way out of the wrecked Datsun.

Since opening the driver's side door above him was virtually impossible, that left only one other way out: through the windshield. Just the thought of trying to shatter the laminated safety glass made him tired; putting any weight at all on his fractured right leg was so painful that it brought on waves of nausea. But how else could he get out?

Ever so gently, Al rolled his hips to the right, until, at last, he was face down across the passenger seat, with his back to the dashboard. Using his left hand, he reached behind him for the glove box, found and pressed the release button, and opened the compartment. There had to be *something* within it that he could use to smash the windshield. He groped around the interior, but felt nothing except some old registration papers and the owner's manual. Wait. What was that? A screwdriver? Yes!

How the hell am I going to crack the windshield with that?

Nevertheless, Al grabbed the screwdriver and pulled it out of the glove box. He held it up where he could see it and smiled. It was a flathead.

At least it's not a Phillips head.

A Phillips head would have been virtually useless, but with the flathead, he just might have a chance at using its sharp flat edge to pry the glass loose from the window frame. If he was *really* lucky, he could do it without cutting himself.

Al laughed aloud. What other choice did he have?

He carefully rolled back to his left, until he was once again facing the dashboard, with the windshield directly above it. The distance to the glass was probably less than three feet, but it might as well have been a mile. Somehow, he needed get off the seat and onto his knees on the floor of the vehicle, so he could begin the arduous task of removing the windshield.

With a monumental effort, Al used his left hand to press against the back of the seat behind him, while simultaneously reaching forward with his right hand, which held the screwdriver. "Oh, God!" he screamed, as the pain from the broken ribs threatened to cause him to lose consciousness. Perspiration dotted his forehead, and he felt nausea beginning to engulf him once more. He fell back against the seatback.

"Too tired," he whispered. "Gotta rest." Then he passed out.

* * * * *

"How the hell am I going to be able to work like this?" Bobcat asked the nurse, looking at his newly bandaged right hand. He'd had to wait nearly an hour before a doctor at the Urgent Care facility examined his burned extremity. He decided that the name Urgent Care was an oxymoron. However, short of driving another half hour to Monticello and waiting twice that long in the emergency room, coming here had probably been his best option.

Bobcat's question had been rhetorical, but the woman answered it just the same. "Well, sir, if I were you I'd take a few days off and just let it heal." Her nametag read: Joyce Hillriegel.

Bobcat smiled. "Well, Joyce, I wish I could. But that wouldn't help me catch the guy who . . . oh, never mind. How long before I can get out of here?"

"Actually, you can leave anytime you want, just as soon as you sign these papers." She handed Bobcat a clipboard with a pen attached to it by a length of string. "Just let me know when you've finished," she added with a warm smile. "I can only imagine how exhausted you must be."

Bobcat smiled in return. "Yeah, well, it *was* kind of a long night and all. But we'll make it."

Twenty minutes later, he had checked out and was on his way back to Roscoe. He could just imagine the razzing he would have to absorb from Nancy and Rick. His throbbing right hand reminded him of the work he had in front of him, and he winced at the thought of what lay in store.

Oh well, the sooner I get back, the sooner I can get this whole thing behind me.

Up ahead, the illuminated sign above the Roscoe Diner served as a beacon, guiding him home.

Coffee. That's what he needed. Lots of coffee—and *maybe* one donut.

Chapter 40

Montana

Jimmy and Henry first saw the flashing lights as they approached the turn-off leading to the road on which the trailers were located.

"Oh, shit," said Jimmy.

"Relax," Henry assured him. "It's probably just an accident."

There were several emergency vehicles on the scene, including a fire truck and a maintenance truck from the local power company. A State Trooper, wearing a reflective safety vest, was directing traffic, his vehicle blocking the entrance to the road. He pointed at their pickup and signaled for them to turn around.

Henry put on his left turn signal, and slowed the pickup to a crawl, finally stopping alongside the police officer. He rolled down his window, but before he could speak, the trooper tipped his hat and informed him, "Sorry, sir, but the road's blocked, and—"

"What happened?"

"Fella had a heart attack and lost control of his vehicle. It'll only be a little while before they—"

"But we live right down there," said Henry, pointing in the direction of Walter's and their trailers. "Can't we just get back to our house?"

"Sorry," apologized the officer, "but the car took out a utility pole, and there are live electric lines across the road. Come on back in an hour or so, and you should be able to get through then."

"Ask him if we can park here and walk back," Jimmy urged.

The trooper leaned in close to the open window of the pickup, his eyes locking on Jimmy's. "I heard that," he said. "I'm afraid that just isn't possible. Now come back in an hour, okay?"

"Yeah, yeah, that's fine," conceded Henry. "No problem. We'll come back then. Thank you very much, officer."

The last thing Henry wanted to do was to get in a shouting match with a cop. He looked in the rearview mirror, saw that there was no one behind their truck, and backed it up about fifty feet. Then, he made a U-turn and headed back toward Johnny's.

"Shit, man," said Jimmy. "Where are you going? We gotta get back home and warn Walter and Ronald."

"Relax," Henry said. "One hour isn't going to make a difference. We'll just go back and spend a little more time with *Ehawee*. Everything's going to be fine."

*   *   *   *   *

Shorty made his way down the hall of the doublewide to the living room, tapping the walls with his fingers as he went, much like an insect uses its antennae as feelers to sense its environment. It wasn't really necessary, however, because after being deprived of light for such a long period of time, his eyes were extra sensitive, and he was able to see relatively well.

He knew that Injun One and Injun Two had gone out earlier, which just left Injun Four unaccounted for. There was no time to waste. He had figured out early on that the older man lived somewhere else. But where that was wasn't clear. No matter. He didn't plan on sticking around long enough to find out.

Opening the front door, Shorty looked around to get his bearings, and to be sure that no one was watching. The fresh night air was a welcome departure from the trailer's stale interior. He breathed deeply, filling his lungs.

There was another trailer toward the rear of the property, and he guessed that was where Injun Four lived—at least he hoped so. The only two vehicles in sight were an old, red Ford pickup that was parked in front of the second building, and a rusted-out Jeep in front of the double wide. Never one for Jeeps, Shorty rifled through the keys on the key ring he'd taken from Ronald until he came across one bearing a Ford logo.

This better be it, or I'm in big trouble.

It wasn't until he stepped off the front porch that he realized he was barefooted. "Screw it," he muttered. He didn't have time to go back for his boots. He made his way across the lot to the pickup, stones and pebbles bruising the undersides of his feet. "Be asleep, old man," he whispered, ignoring the pain. "Just be asleep."

The truck was unlocked, and Shorty carefully opened the door and climbed in.

"Jesus," he whispered. "What the hell is that smell?"

He looked around the interior of the Ford until he located the source of the odor. It was a white, cardboard container half-filled with rotting Chinese food, or at least that's what it appeared to be. He reached behind the seat, grabbed the container, and flung it out the open window of the truck.

He inserted the key into the ignition and fired up the old V-8. The engine ran like crap, but it was the sweetest sound he'd heard in all his life. He turned on the lights and shifted into reverse, backed up a bit, and put the automatic transmission into drive. He tromped down on the accelerator and headed off the property and onto the road, before coming to a screeching halt on the macadam.

He had no idea where he was, nor did he have a clue as to which direction he should drive. To make matters worse, when he glanced at the fuel gauge, he saw that the needle was hugging the E. Shorty flipped a coin mentally, and decided to make a right.

"Fuck it!" he cried. "At least I'm free. Road's gotta go *somewhere* better than this."

Then, just as he turned and was starting down the highway, he looked in the rear view mirror and saw the lights in both trailers came on in unison. He pressed harder on the accelerator, and soon saw the analog speedometer's needle nudging the seventy-miles-per-hour mark. He didn't know exactly where he was headed, but he was making good time.

He hadn't driven more than five minutes when a pair of headlights shown in the rearview mirror. Shorty took a quick peek, and was relieved to see that the vehicle they belonged to was well off in the distance. However, several more glances confirmed his worst fears. Whoever was driving, was driving even faster than he was—and they were closing fast.

*   *   *   *   *

Matt and Chris were feeling energized. It was almost like old times. Ever since Matt had made the decision to quit fishing and stop worrying about the possible consequences, he had grown more optimistic about their chances for success. He definitely preferred being proactive—even if it *was* on a somewhat limited basis.

Now, as they headed back out to Johnny's to put the screws to "Pocahontas," ideas and theories were bouncing back and forth between the two ex-partners like steel balls inside a pinball machine. The only things missing were the sound effects and flashing lights.

"I've been thinking a lot about this," offered Matt. "The very fact that these guys are staying in touch gives me hope. I think they're a bunch of small time operators who saw a chance for some easy money, and now they're in over their heads."

Chris laughed. "You mean like the gang that couldn't shoot straight?" (He was referring, of course, to the book written by Jimmy Breslin that was subsequently made into a highly successful motion picture.)

"Yeah. Kinda. And that would be great, except for one thing," suggested Matt. "They're very, *very* unpredictable.

Either they all turn on one another and everything kind of falls apart — or, they go down with guns blazing."

"Yeah, don't remind me," Chris agreed.

"Am I right?"

"I'm afraid so."

"Well, let's hope it's the former."

They rode the rest of the way to Johnny's in silence.

Chapter 41

Roscoe, NY

Nancy Cooper looked at the office clock hanging above her desk. It read 11:50. Just ten minutes more and she'd be able to take her lunch break. She could hardly wait. She glanced over at the collection of travel brochures stacked neatly on the seat of the spare visitors chair in the corner and smiled. Every single one was about England. She'd made up her mind. The minute Matt returned from Montana, she'd give her notice.

Her reverie was broken by the sound of the phone. She picked it up on the second ring. It was Mayor Swenson.

"Oh, hi, Harold. What can I do for you?"

Harold Swenson was not one to mince words. When he had a point to make, he usually got straight to it. "For starters, you can tell me when Matt's coming back?"

Nancy started to answer, then paused. His Honor wasn't exactly her favorite person, and passive aggression was her middle name. So, he could wait.

"Hello? Nancy? Are you there?"

"Oh, I'm sorry, Harold. You were saying?"

"I asked when Matt is coming back."

"Well, I think he left his itinerary here someplace. Can you hang on a minute? Or would you rather I call you back?"

The clock now read 11:55.

"Oh, never mind," Harold said. "I think I have a copy of it somewhere, too. Actually, I just wanted to know if you'd heard from him."

"*Actually*, no," replied Nancy. "But I'll certainly tell him you were asking, next time he calls."

"Yeah, you do that. Oh, and tell him I've got some bad news."

"Really? And what might that be?"

"It's about Frank Kuttner."

"What *about* Frank Kuttner? Is he okay?" (Frank owned a fly shop in Livingston Manor, and was a good friend of Matt's.)

"He's fine," replied Harold. "He's just going out of business."

"He is?"

"Uh huh," confided the mayor. "Talked to him the other night at a Chamber of Commerce meeting. He's decided enough is enough. He's packing it in."

"Matt won't be happy about that," Nancy acknowledged. "Do you want *me* to tell him, or would you rather deliver the bad news yourself?"

"Either way," replied the mayor. "He'll probably take it better if he hears it from you."

"Okay. I'll tell him . . . uh . . . *when* I speak to him again, of course." Nancy glanced up at the clock. "Oh, oh, you'll have to excuse me, Harold. It's noon. Time for lunch."

"Okay, okay," Harold conceded. "I wouldn't want to keep you from the trough."

Nancy drummed her fingers on the desk, refusing to rise to the bait.

"Sorry," laughed Harold. "I just couldn't resist."

More drumming.

"Okay, well, just tell Matt to give me a call, will ya?"

"Have a nice day, Harold."

*   *   *   *   *

Val Davis looked at the calendar hanging from the colorful fish magnet on the side of the refrigerator. It had been four days since she last spoke to Matt, and exactly a week since he'd left home. A large, penciled X filled the box of each day that Matt had been gone. Just seven days, but it felt like a month. In all the years they'd been married, this was only the second time they had been apart this long. Ironically, it was also Montana that had come between them before.

She knew he must be missing her at least as much as she missed him. But that knowledge was scarcely comforting. She picked up the receiver on the wall phone and punched in his cell phone number. Without ringing, the call was immediately routed to his voice mail. She listened intently to the recorded message that asked the caller to "please leave your name, phone number, and a brief message, and I will return your call as soon as possible. And thanks for calling."

Hearing Matt's voice buoyed Val's spirits and brought a brief smile to her face. For just an instant, she felt like a schoolgirl, and she felt herself flush.

After all these years, she thought, he could still make her blush.

You sexy devil.

*   *   *   *   *

Bobcat sat down at his desk and contemplated his computer screen. A collection of *National Geographic* photographs were laid out in a neat checkerboard design across its face. Reluctantly, he picked up the wireless mouse with his left hand, and pressed the left button. Immediately, the screensaver disappeared and an array of icons representing various folders and Internet links came into view. He right-clicked on the one for Mozilla Firefox and selected "Open" from the drop-down list of options. Once the browser loaded, he selected the tab for the New York Division of Motor Vehicles, and clicked on it.

Using his left index finger, he carefully typed in the user name and password that he, as a law enforcement officer, possessed to access the database. Twice, he hit an incorrect key, and had to start all over again. Finally, he was ready to search.

From his shirt pocket, he withdrew the sheet of paper containing the license plate number of the blue Datsun, unfolded it, and placed it on the desk. He hit the "Caps Lock" key on the keyboard, slowly and deliberately entered the combination of three letters and four numbers into the search window, and clicked on the search icon.

Almost instantaneously, the data appeared on the screen. It showed the Datsun registered to an Al Coif, at 2218 Elm Hollow Road, in Livingston Manor.

Bobcat minimized the window, clicked on Word, and opened a new, blank document. Then, he brought the website window back up and right-clicked to copy the information. He minimized the window again and pasted the data into the Word document, and hit print.

He smiled smugly and thought, *not bad for a one-armed cop*, then exited the website and retrieved the printed piece of paper from the wireless printer in the corner of the room. He walked into Nancy's office to tell her he was leaving, but her cubicle was empty.

He whistled softly as he left headquarters and headed toward his vehicle. Won't Matt be proud, he thought, as he fired up the Pathfinder.

Next stop, Livingston Manor.

Chapter 42

Montana

As soon as he realized that he was being chased, Shorty trounced down on the accelerator and stayed on it until the needle on the speedometer hit ninety. Pretty soon, the headlights in the rearview mirror had disappeared, and Shorty turned off his own. Owing to a nearly full moon, however, he could still see the road in front of him, just not as well as before. He dared not push the pickup any faster, because, if he did, there was a good chance he might hit a stray animal. Hitting a deer, or, worse yet, a cow, at high speed wouldn't be pretty; he was already in enough danger.

The landscape was pretty barren in every direction. Typical southwest Montana terrain. Shorty scanned the horizon, looking for a side road down which he could turn and hopefully find a hiding place. Just as he was losing hope, he spotted the beginning of some barbed-wire fencing on the left side of the road. He slowed the pickup by half, and kept it at that speed until he saw an ornate set of gates, attached to some fancy masonry. There was a large sign above the gates announcing the name of the spread: Triple Delight Ranch. It was a name he was familiar with. At least now, he had some idea of where he was.

He pulled the pickup into the cut in the road and stopped just short of the gates. He was in luck. The wrought-iron doors were largely ornamental, and only a hasp and pin arrangement with no padlock held them together. He threw the transmission into park and exited the vehicle. He pushed against the right-hand gate, and kept pushing until there was an opening large enough for the truck to pass through.

He looked back along the main road, but saw no sign of the headlights belonging to the following vehicle. There was no time to waste. Jumping back into the pickup, Shorty threw the transmission into drive and drove through the opening. He quickly stopped again, ran back and closed the gate, then re-entered the pickup and started driving as fast as he dared, hoping to find help ahead.

He hadn't gone more than a couple of hundred yards when the engine hesitated, sputtered along for a bit, and then shut down completely. He threw the transmission into park, pumped the accelerator several times, and turned the ignition key. The engine coughed, ran for three or four seconds, and quit again.

"Shit!"

He dropped his head down close to the instrument cluster and looked at the gas gauge. The needle was resting below the E. He tapped the glass several times, but the needle wouldn't budge. He was out of gas.

Now what?

*   *   *   *   *

Matt pulled the rental car into the dirt parking lot at Johnny's. There were two vehicles parked in the far corner. One was the pink Volkswagen they had seen before (which he had correctly guessed belonged to the barmaid), and the other was a nondescript Chevy pickup belonging to a previous decade.

"Greetings, Pocahontas," said Chris, as they entered the front door. "Glad to see us?"

Janice had a bar rag in her hand, and appeared intent upon ignoring the duo, as she continued polishing several beer mugs without acknowledging them.

Off to Chris's right, the same two elderly Native American patrons who had been there previously frowned their disapproval at the politically incorrect language.

"Fuck you," mouthed Chris, as he smiled at the two men and tipped his hat. Matt nudged his partner in the ribs, as if to say "enough," then walked over to where Janice was practically removing the shine from the glass beer steins. He tipped his western-style hat and offered a thin apology for Chris's insensitive behavior, just in case the girl had overheard his partner.

"My friend is actually part Mohawk," he explained. "He thinks it gives him the right to say whatever comes to mind. I apologize for the two of us. I hope you weren't offended."

Janice smiled. "I've heard worse," confessed the girl. "So, what brings you back here so soon?"

Once again, Matt pulled out his police badge, only this time he didn't put it away. He held it out for the young girl to see.

"Okay, so you're a cop. Big deal. We get cops in here all the time. It doesn't cut any ice with me. Frankly, I couldn't care less."

"I think you might care this time," Matt suggested. "*Especially* when I tell you why we're here."

"And *why* exactly *are* you here?" asked Janice.

"We're investigating a kidnapping," answered Chris.

Janice's lips grew tight, and all the color drained from her face. Still, she said nothing.

"Did you hear what he said?" Matt asked.

"I heard him."

"Well, that's the *good* news," Chris said.

"The *bad* news is," Matt advised her, "that if anything happens to the fellow who was kidnapped, and if it turns out that you knew something about it and didn't tell us, you could be in some pretty serious trouble."

"And, if by some chance, he were to be killed," added Chris, "you could be looking at the electric chair."

"All right, all right," Matt cautioned his partner, "don't go scaring the poor girl to death."

By now there was no disguising the emotion coursing through the young barmaid's veins. She was scared. Her hands were trembling almost uncontrollably as she tried to control her fear.

"So, I ask you," Matt said, "would you like to rethink what you told us earlier?"

"Yeah," said Chris. "Have you noticed any fellow *landsmen*, for lack of a better term, throwing money around like drunken sailors?"

Janice paused wiping the beer mugs. She appeared to be on the verge of making a decision.

"We're talking death penalty, here," Chris said. "You do *not* want to be hiding anything from us—especially not now."

The young woman put her hands on her hips, took a deep breath, and exhaled. "Look," she said, at last, "I don't want any trouble. But what if I give you their names and they're *not* the kidnappers? I mean, I *need* this job. No one will ever trust me again. This isn't exactly the employment capital of Montana here, in case you haven't noticed. What about *that*?"

Matt could certainly understand the girl's predicament, and he surely didn't want to cost her her job. But he also knew the clock was ticking, and a man's life might possibly be at stake.

"Look, Miss. I can't guarantee your job, but I *can* guarantee what will happen if you know something and don't share what you know with us. I'll do everything in my power to see that you stay employed."

"Is there a reward?"

"Nope," replied Chris.

"But," chimed in Matt, "I imagine that the man who we're looking for might be able to persuade his boss to come up with a little something as a token of appreciation for getting his ranch foreman back alive. No promises, but I'd see what we could do."

Chris nodded in agreement.

"Okay," whispered Janice. "I'll tell you what. Come back here after I close at midnight, and I'll tell you what you want to know then." With a subtle nod of her head, she motioned toward her only two customers down at the end of the bar. "I don't want to take any chances that *somebody* might overhear me talking to you."

"Agreed," said Matt. "I understand completely."

In a loud voice, Janice informed Matt and Chris, "Okay, then. I'll see if I can get you two lined up with a genuine Indian hunting guide who can show you around the area. I can't promise that you'll actually get to shoot anything. That'll be up to you."

Chris tipped his Stetson. "Well, we'd be most obliged if you could hook us up."

"Yep," agreed Matt. "We sure would appreciate it. We'll check back tomorrow, okay?"

"You got it," said Janice. "See you then."

Matt and Chris turned and started toward the entrance to the bar.

"Obliged?" whispered Matt to his partner. "Did you actually say *obliged*?"

"Oh, fuck you and the horse you rode in on," laughed Chris.

The two men exited the front door, climbed into their rental vehicle, and headed back to Big Sky Fin and Fur.

As Janice watched them leave, she began examining her options. No matter how she played it over in her mind, she was screwed. If she didn't tell the two officers about her Indian friends, a man's death could end up on her conscience. If she talked, and it turned out that it was someone else responsible, she'd have a hard time explaining to any of the Native Americans who frequented Johnny's that she could ever be trusted again.

* * * * *

When Jimmy and Henry pulled up to Johnny's, the only car in the lot was Janice's hideous pink Volkswagen. Jimmy felt a tightness in his groin, as he pictured the young Indian girl's curvaceous figure. Maybe, when all this was over and he had some *real* money in his pocket, he could spend a lot more time with *Ehawee*.

"Well, well," Janice said when she saw the two come through the front door, "what are you two doing back so soon?"

"Didn't have any choice," Henry informed her. "Some pea-brained drunk hit a pole near our trailer, and took out the power lines. State police wouldn't let us through."

"Well," replied Janice, "I guess this isn't your lucky night, I'm afraid. I was just about to close up the place."

Jimmy looked at his wristwatch. The digital display said nine fifty-eight. "It's not even ten o'clock yet?" he complained. "I thought you usually stay open until midnight. What gives?"

"What *gives*," Janice answered, "is that I haven't had a customer in here since you guys left. Boss always tells me if it's ten o'clock and you haven't had a customer in the last hour, close it up. So, that's what I'm doing."

With a hint of adventure in his voice, Jimmy suggested, "Well, go ahead and close up, *Ehawee*. We'll just hang out until you're ready to—"

"Close?" Janice said, finishing his sentence. "Sorry, Jimmy, but I can't have anybody in here when I close."

"I think what he means," suggested Henry, "is why don't you just lock the door and we'll have us a little party?"

"Look," Janice insisted, "I don't think that's a good idea. Besides, you really should be looking at getting out of town."

"Whoa!" replied Jimmy. "Where did *that* come from?"

Janice bit the bullet. "Okay, look. You remember those two guys I told you about before?"

"Yeah, I remember," Henry said. "The insurance investigators, right?"

"Yeah, well they came back after you left. They're *not* insurance investigators. They're cops."

"Are you sure?"

"Yep. And they're looking for you—*and* probably Ronald and Walter, too, I would imagine. What have you guys gone and done? Who'd you kidnap?"

"Kidnap?"

"Well, isn't that what you've done? I knew there was something funny going on the minute you flashed that fifty-dollar bill."

Neither Henry nor Jimmy was denying the accusation, and that only served to convince Janice that the two cops were telling the truth.

"Did you tell them anything?" inquired Henry.

"No, of course not," Janice told them. She could say that with conviction, because she'd yet to divulge anything to the two lawmen. "What could I have told them? I don't *know* anything. And that's the way I'd prefer to leave it. So, please, for everybody's sake, just go, okay?"

"Maybe you ought to come with us?" suggested Henry.

"Oh, yeah. What're you gonna do, kidnap me, too?"

"Relax," said Jimmy. "Nobody's kidnapping anybody. Maybe you're right, *Ehawee*. Maybe we need to get lost for a while. Thanks for the heads-up."

Janice breathed a sigh of relief. "You're welcome, I guess. Now, please leave, so I can close up this damn place. *Please*."

"Yeah, yeah. We're leaving," Henry replied. "Ain't that right, Jimmy?"

"Yeah. And don't tell those fellows anything. Okay?"

Janice was silent.

"I said, ain't that right, Ehawee?"

"I won't say a word," replied Janice. "Now please, can you just leave?"

"We're outta here," Jimmy announced.

Henry waved over his shoulder, as the pair made their way out the door.

As soon as she heard the pickup pull out of the parking lot, Janice rushed to the door and locked it. The two lawmen would be back in less than two hours. In the meantime, she had work to do—and plans to make.

Chapter 43

Roscoe, NY

If you look at a map of New York State, it appears that the town of Roscoe is nothing more than a dot in the far west corner of Sullivan County—and that's fairly accurate. In reality, however, Roscoe isn't even a town; it's a hamlet. Along with thirteen other hamlets, it is located within the sprawling piece of geography known as the town of Rockland. Head northwest on Route 206, and you'll leave Sullivan County, and cross into Delaware County. Head east, and you'll come to Livingston Manor, which was where Bobcat was headed.

As he drove his Pathfinder east along Old Route 17, he marveled at the gin-clear water of Willowemoc Creek, which flowed west on the south side of the road toward its confluence with the Beaverkill at Junction Pool in Roscoe. Unlike Matt, he had never wet a line, and had no interest in trout fishing, but he could surely appreciate the beauty of the waters the sleek fish inhabited. Presently, however, the only thing on his mind was finding and arresting the man responsible for the recent spate of fires that had caused so much anxiety and damage in the area.

He passed Hazel Bridge Road on his right, then Judy Van Put's real estate office on his left, and continued on past Amber Lake Road. Up ahead, in the distance, on the right, he could see the fishermen's parking area and the road that ran across the small bridge over the Willowemoc to the Catskill Fly Fishing Center and Museum. It was rare that there weren't at least a half dozen vehicles parked by the water, and today was no exception. Bobcat chuckled as he passed the pool by the bridge, and, without thinking, instinctively tooted his horn at the fishermen working the waters above and below it.

"Ouch!" he cried, as his burned right hand struck the surface of the steering wheel. The pain was excruciating. Hopefully, the antibiotics he'd been given at Urgent Care would keep the wound from becoming infected, but not even the heavy bandages could totally protect him from his own stupidity. He grimaced at the pain, and made a mental note to be more careful.

Just before the intersection of Beaverkill Road and Old Route 17, Bobcat took a shortcut and maneuvered the Pathfinder in front of the old abandoned building that sat at the corner. Kuttner's Fly Shop was not far ahead on the left. Were it not for the hand-painted sign out front, it would be easy to miss the outbuilding, which sat to the rear of Frank's residence, and Bob wondered how people ever found the little business. Blink once, he thought, and you'd miss it. Blink twice, and you'd never know it ever existed. It was hard to imagine it closing, but easy to understand the reasoning behind the decision.

Elm Hollow Road was another mile or so up on the right, just before the two Rockland municipal buildings that sat on the left side of the road: one a transfer station, the other a highway department edifice. Bobcat flipped on his right directional, and gingerly shifted the automatic transmission into "low," as he made the turn. Whereas Beaverkill Road was fully paved, Elm Hollow Road was only partially surfaced, and not very user friendly. Over the course of its length, it formed a huge loop that eventually took it back to Beaverkill Road—after several miles and countless hundreds of potholes. According to the map, the address Bobcat was looking for, number 2218, was just about at the midpoint of the circle.

Since the house numbers were directly related to the distance from the nearest intersection—a system designed to assist first responders—it was easy to find the address by using the Pathfinder's odometer. A dilapidated, metal mailbox, with reflective numerals affixed to its wooden post, marked the driveway that led up to the old farmhouse. Bobcat drove the Pathfinder slowly up the overgrown gravel driveway, throwing up clouds of dust as he made his way past an abandoned chicken coop and a rundown outbuilding.

The main house was a mess. Stacks of newspapers lined the front porch, and an old International Harvester tractor stood sentinel alongside the dwelling; obviously, it was in no condition to move. Sad, thought Bobcat. A fine piece of machinery like that, gone to waste. At one time, this farm probably supported a family, perhaps even with something to spare. Now, it stood as a reminder of the changing economy of the area. Farming was dying out, and tourism and gentrification was taking its place. Neither industry was in evidence at this location, however. And neither was the blue Datsun.

"Shit," whispered Bobcat. "I should have known it wouldn't be *that* easy."

He pulled the pathfinder alongside the tractor, shifting the transmission into park, and leaving the motor running as he exited the SUV. A soft rain was just beginning to fall.

There was a bell located next to the front door, and he pulled the piece of rawhide attached to it several times, eliciting a loud clanging that should have been sufficient to raise the dead.

But no one responded.

He waited a minute or so before repeating the process.

"Anybody home?" he called.

No answer.

After several more attempts, it became apparent that there was no one present. Bobcat, made his way down off the porch, and slowly wandered around the perimeter of the house. He didn't really know what he was looking for, other than the blue Datsun, but he felt he ought to look just the same.

Maybe I should just hang out here for a while and see what happens.

There was a barn in the rear that looked as if it might have housed some livestock at one time. It was empty of course, but could certainly provide cover for someone eluding law enforcement. With that in mind, Bobcat slowly and carefully withdrew his service weapon from its holster, and made his way toward the building.

"Anyone here?" he called, as he approached the barn doors.

No answer.

Using his good left hand, he opened one of the doors and stepped inside. Nothing but some hay and a few rusted attachments for the tractor. He backed out and closed the door. The rain had gone from a shower to a deluge. Bobcat shielded his face with his good hand.

What am I wasting my time for? There's nobody here.

"Mister Coif?" he called out.

Nothing.

Okay, that's it. I'm not wasting one more minute.

As he turned to go, a muffled bark behind him nearly caused him to drop his weapon. He turned and looked back in the direction of the barn. There, to the right, stood an old collie dog, its wet coat ragged and covered with nettles. Bobcat approached the animal and, putting his weapon back into its holster, reached out with his good hand to pat its head. "Good boy," he said. "Good boy."

The dog cocked its head and studied Bobcat. "Woof! Woof!" Its voice was as ragged as its coat.

"Where's your master, boy?"

"Woof!"

"Yeah," said Bobcat with a laugh. "I feel exactly the same."

What an idiot, he thought. There he was, standing in the pouring rain, talking to a dog—and expecting it to answer him.

"That's it," he said aloud. "I'm outta here."

*   *   *   *   *

The first few drops of rain dripped gently through the open driver's side window of the Datsun and onto Al Coif's bare head, rousing him from a deep and troubled sleep. He swiveled his head to face upward, opened his mouth, and caught some of the precious liquid on his tongue. It was like manna from Heaven. Groping around the interior of the car, he located an empty beer bottle, and attempted to catch as much of the rain as he could. It was clear, however, that this method was not sufficient to his needs.

Looking around, Al spotted the empty pizza box lying on the passenger seat. He reached out for it and was hit with a searing pain from his fractured ribs. He screamed, which brought on even more pain. After what seemed like an eternity, he managed to reach the box, and tore a piece of cardboard from its top, which he carefully formed into the shape of a funnel. He inserted the makeshift funnel into the neck of the empty beer bottle and smiled.

Much better.

Al held the jury-rigged contraption up to the open window, and, before long, he had collected enough rainwater to nearly fill the glass container. He removed the cardboard and drank greedily from the bottle, suckling it like a newborn baby might do at its mother's breast. As long as he didn't move too much, his broken ribs were not a problem. But the minute he had to stretch or turn, the pain would come roaring back.

Gradually the tempo of the rain increased, and before long Al wished he'd closed the window the night before. Closing it now, however, was out of the question, so he did the best he could to protect himself away from the stream of rainwater that was cascading into the car. Whoever said you could never get too much of a good thing had never been in Al's predicament.

Using his left leg, he pushed ever so gently against the bottom of the driver's side door, which permitted his pelvis to slide down the seat and away from the stream of rainwater. The effort, however, was not without consequence, as a new wave of pain washed over him when his fractured right leg struck the passenger side door. He gritted his teeth and struggled not to scream, but the pain was so intense that he couldn't stop himself.

"Aaaaarghhhh!"

As he screamed, his broken ribs responded in kind, thereby doubling the intensity of his discomfort. Tears rolled down his cheeks and mixed with the rainwater already soaking his shirt. To make matters worse, the air temperature, which had been fairly comfortable, had begun to drop precipitously with the onset of the rain. Now, it was downright cold.

Al began to shiver uncontrollably, which brought on even more pain. Eventually, his body could no longer endure the discomfort, and he drifted off into unconsciousness.

Time was running out.

Chapter 44

Montana

Walter Begay was in full panic mode. He had been watching TV when the lights had gone out, and his first thoughts had been directed at the Vigilante Electric Cooperative that served southwestern Montana.

Damn power company.

They were just getting ready to announce the semifinalists on the music competition show he'd been watching, and he was pissed.

Why can't it go out when I'm sleeping?

Intermittent power outages were frequent in rural Montana, and Walter had no doubt that the lights would be back on in a minute or two. So he sat in the dark and waited.

When power hadn't been restored within a few minutes, however, he began thinking about the prisoner. Maybe it wasn't the cooperative to blame after all. Maybe Ronald had screwed up somehow, and the prisoner he'd been guarding had escaped and was on the loose. Maybe *he* had turned off the power.

Could it be?

When he heard the starter motor of the pickup turning over the Ford's engine, his greatest fears were realized. He rose from the recliner he'd been sitting in, and groped blindly on the snack table beside it for his keys. The trailer was pitch black, and it took more time than he would have liked to make his way to the front door. As he did, the headlights of the truck swept across the yard, and Walter could see the silhouette of the man behind the wheel. It definitely wasn't Ronald.

"Ronald!" he shouted, as he ran out the front door toward the doublewide. "What the hell happened?"

When he saw that the front door was open, his heart sank. All he could think of was how he would spend the rest of his miserable life behind bars if he couldn't catch their prisoner. "Goddamn it, Ronald," he shouted. "I'm too friggin' old for this!"

He made his way slowly through the interior of the trailer until he came upon Ronald's unconscious body in the middle of the floor in the hallway. He knelt down and felt for a pulse. It was strong and steady. At least the boy was alive, he thought.

"Ronald," he called, "wake up!" He patted the young man's cheek, gently at first, then harder. "Wake up!"

Ronald groaned and reached his hand up to his neck, which was swollen from the headlock Shorty had applied to it when the lights had gone out. "Walter," he whispered. "I think he got away. I'm sorry. I screwed up bad."

"How did it happen? Is *he* the one who turned off the power?"

"No. No. I was taking him to the bathroom, I was holding onto the chain, just the way I always do . . . and everything was just fine . . . and then . . . the lights went out. And that's all I remember."

"Can you stand up?"

"I think so."

Walter took hold of the young Indian's arm and helped him to his feet. As he did, he noticed that Ronald's hands were cuffed. "Where're your keys?" he asked.

"I don't know. He must've took 'em."

"Shit."

"Don't you have another key?" Ronald asked.

"Yeah, but it's in my trailer. Stay here. I'll be right back."

Five minutes later, Walter was back with the key, and he unlocked the cuffs, freeing Ronald's hands.

"Let's go!" Walter barked. "We've got to find him."

"Should I bring the rifle?"

"Never mind that. I've got mine in the jeep."

The two men hurried out the open front door of the doublewide and climbed into Walter's Jeep. In less than thirty seconds, they were headed down the road. Walter didn't know which way Shorty had gone, but he was hoping he guessed correctly when he turned right onto the highway.

The Jeep's speedometer topped out at 85, and the needle was buried. The front end of the ancient vehicle shimmied wildly, but Walter kept the accelerator pressed to the floor. In a few minutes, the glow from another vehicle's taillights could be seen up ahead.

"That's gotta be him," Walter said.

"I sure hope you're right," said Ronald.

"If it isn't, we're screwed. We might as well keep on driving — right on down to Mexico."

"I've never been to Mexico," Ronald confessed.

"Oh, shut up, you idiot. We're not going to Mexico. We're gonna catch that son of a bitch, and everything's gonna be fine." *Or we're all going to jail.*

Walter squinted, peering into the darkness and desperately trying to make out whether or not the vehicle in front of him was a red Ford truck.

"We're gaining on him . . . I think," Ronald suggested.

"No doubt about it," Walter agreed. "That old Ford'll blow a gasket if he keeps pushin' it like that. Don't worry, we'll catch him."

Then the taillights in front of them disappeared.

*   *   *   *   *

Matt looked at his watch. It had been an hour and a half since they'd left the bar. "I think it's time we head back out to Johnny's, don't you think?"

There was no answer from Chris. Matt looked over at his partner, to where he was sitting in the overstuffed chair by the fireplace, and saw why. Chris was dead asleep.

Matt stood up, walked over, and gently kicked Chris's shoe with the toe of his own. "Wake up, sleepyhead. It's time to go."

Most cops have an innate ability to sleep in short fits and starts whenever an opportunity presents itself. It might be said that Chris Freitag wrote the book on the subject. They also have the knack of being able to rouse themselves almost instantaneously when necessary.

"Yeah, okay, let's do it," Chris responded. "You want me to drive?"

"Nah, that's okay. I'll drive. You can get some more sleep on the way over. It's obvious you *need* it."

"Fuck you," Chris said. "You're older than I am. *You* sleep. I'll drive."

"Whatever."

Twenty minutes later, Chris pulled the rental car into the lot at Johnny's, stopping right by the front door. The interior of the bar was dark. Janice's pink Volkswagen was where it had been when they left, down at the end of the parking lot. There were no other vehicles in evidence.

"You think she flew the coop?" Chris asked.

"Not if she's smart. I'll check the front door. You look and see if she's in the VW."

Matt ascended the brick steps leading up to the front door, and knocked hard. Glancing over at the window immediately to his right, he detected movement within the bar. "She's inside," he called to Chris.

Turning back, he was greeted by Janice, who had unlocked and opened the door. She wore a pained expression, one that revealed both fear and annoyance.

Chris joined Matt, and the two entered the bar, with Janice quickly closing and locking the door behind them.

"Okay," she began, "what do you want to know?"

"Well," Matt replied, "for starters, how many men are we talking about?"

Janice hesitated. It was obvious to Matt that the girl was conflicted.

"Look, whether you give us one name or ten, it won't make any difference," Matt assured her. "The important thing is that we save a man's life—and you save your own ass—to put it bluntly. Now how about it?"

"Okay, okay," Janice began. "There's four of them that pretty much hang together, so I—"

"Names," Matt said. "I need *names*."

"Well, there's Walter Begay. He's a Blackfeet—and he's kind of an old man. Then there's Ronald White Feather—he's a Flathead and—"

"Skip the biographies," Matt barked. "I couldn't care less what tribes they belong to. Just give me the other two names." He was growing impatient.

"Jimmy Blackwater and Henry Golden Eagle," Janice answered with a frown. "Satisfied?"

"And where can we find them?" Chris asked.

Janice smiled. "That's the good part," she said. "They all live together. Well, not *exactly*. Walter lives behind the other three in his own trailer. But they all—"

"What's the address?" Matt asked.

Janice rolled her eyes. "I don't know the address, silly. What do I look like, a phone directory?"

"But you *do* know where they live, right?" Chris asked.

"Well, of course."

"Then tell us how to get there—*now!*" Matt ordered.

"Or, better yet, *show* us," suggested Chris. "We'll follow you there."

"No way!" cried Janice. "I'm not taking any chances they could see me with you. Forget that!"

"All right," conceded Matt, "you can stay here. Just hurry up and tell us how to get there."

"Well," Janice said, "as I started to say, Walter lives in a trailer behind the double-wide where the other three live."

"Is it on a main road?" Chris asked.

"Well, almost. It's right off Forty One. If you head back toward Dillon, you'll come to a big pond on your left. Just past the pond, also on the left is a dirt road. Take that road to the end, and you'll see the two trailers."

"What's the name of the road?" Matt asked.

"Hell, I don't know. It's the only one there—just past the pond on the—"

"I know," said Chris. "On the left."

"Right," said Janice. "Uh . . . I mean, yeah, correct. It's on the left."

"Okay," Matt interrupted. "Are we through with the geography lesson?"

"Oh, one other thing," said Chris. "Do you think these are the kind of guys who might carry guns?"

Matt winced.

Janice smiled.

"This is Montana," she laughed. "What do *you* think?"

"Sorry I asked."

Chapter 45

Roscoe, NY

As Bobcat drove away from the farm, he let his mind wander a bit. Maybe the blue Datsun wasn't there because its owner never made it back the previous night. After all, Coif *had* been drunk.

Who knows, maybe he had an accident?

All kinds of scenarios flooded in and out of his mind. He tried to think the way Matt would if he were there. What *would* Matt do?

He'd be calling every hospital in the area.

So Bobcat decided to return to headquarters and start making some phone calls. The rain was really coming down now, and, as he drove, he had to really concentrate to see the road. By the time he reached Stewart Avenue in Roscoe, some of the catch basins were beginning to overflow, and fishermen who'd been chased off the river by the downpour were flooding into the tackle shops that lined the main street of the little town.

An hour later, after calling every hospital within fifty miles of Roscoe *and* every wrecking outfit he could think of that operated in the area, Bobcat was stumped. He scanned the police reports for any arrests the night before, but saw nothing pertaining to his suspect. He decided to take a ride back out to the site of the crime.

A criminal always returns to the scene of the crime.

Maybe the arsonist would return, he thought, just like they did in the movies.

Fat chance!

Twenty minutes later, Bobcat pulled up in front of the burned-out structure on DuCoff Road. Yellow, crime scene tape was draped around the perimeter of what was once a barn. He parked the Pathfinder, turned off the ignition, and got out. He walked toward the skeleton of the burned-out building, looking for something — *anything* — that might provide a clue to the location of the missing blue Datsun.

When he got to where he had found Al Coif's unconscious body, he stopped.

This is stupid.

Then, he thought of Occam's razor, the philosophical concept that posited that the simplest, most obvious answer is often the correct choice. Coif had been drunk. *That* was a fact. What happens to drunks who drive? They usually end up in an accident, in a hospital, or in jail. Coif hadn't been arrested, and he wasn't in any of the local hospitals. There weren't any reports of accidents. But that didn't mean he didn't have one.

What if he *did* have one and he didn't walk away from it? Maybe he hit a deer? Maybe he drove into a tree?

The possibilities were endless.

Bobcat hopped back into the Pathfinder and started the engine. He'd retrace the route from the site of the fire all the way back to Coif's farm. Only he wouldn't be looking for the Datsun. He'd be looking for signs of an accident.

Things were looking up.

*　*　*　*　*

Unfortunately, things were going in the wrong direction for Al Coif. The rain had soaked the interior of the little Datsun, and his wet clothing clung to him like a shroud. The beginning of hypothermia was causing him to shiver uncontrollably, which sent waves of pain coursing through his body, as his fractured ribs and broken leg competed with his lacerated liver for attention. His abdomen was swollen and tender, and his pulse was growing weaker and more rapid. If he didn't get help soon, he'd die right where he lay.

*　*　*　*　*

As he made his way slowly back toward Roscoe, Bobcat scanned both sides of the road, looking for signs of an accident. Rugged fir trees mixed with old-growth hardwoods on either side of the sparsely populated countryside. Most of the land to his right was owned by the state, and was part of the New York State watershed that provided most of the drinking water for New York City.

Along the way, he noted several scarred trees, but none that appeared to have been injured recently. Then, as he was rounding a particularly steep curve, he saw it: several small white pines to his right had been crushed. He slowed the Pathfinder to a crawl, then to a stop on the side of the road. Rain beat a steady tattoo on the hood of the vehicle, and the thought of going out in it caused Bobcat to hesitate, but only for a second.

"Oh, shit," he muttered, as he exited the vehicle, rain immediately running down inside the collar of his tunic. At first, he scrunched up his shoulders against the watery invasion, then relented. "Screw it. If I'm gonna get wet, might as well get good and wet."

Looking down at the wet asphalt, he could just make out the distinct pattern of skid marks heading off toward the shoulder of the road. But there was no mistaking them for anything other than what they were—and they were pointed right at the crumpled white pines. Further inspection of the grass leading up to the trees showed two tire tracks heading straight toward the slope that bordered the reservoir down below.

I sure hope he didn't go in the water, he thought. Pepacton Reservoir was one of the deepest bodies of water in the state, with sections measuring as much as 160 feet in depth.

Now, as Bobcat made his way down the hill, there were more crushed and broken limbs of low hanging white pines, most of which had been planted by the state for soil retention. Bobcat estimated he was at least one or more football field lengths from the road above when he thought he saw a flicker of blue in the distance. Rain was soaking his tunic and the T-shirt beneath it, and even the waistband of his undershorts was beginning to wick moisture from the garments above.

And then, there it was, straight ahead — the blue Datsun. Its undercarriage was fully exposed, and Bobcat could see that the only thing keeping the little car from tumbling the rest of the way down the slope and into the water was a lone oak tree, against which the car rested.

"Hello," called Bobcat. "Anybody in there?"

*　*　*　*　*

At first, Al thought he was hearing things. The sound of the heavy rain beating on the sheet metal of the car played funny tricks on one's hearing, and several times previously, he had mistaken the sound of the falling water for something other than what it was.

This time, however, when he heard the sound again, and there was no mistaking its origin.

"Help," he shouted, only it came out more like a whisper. "I'm in here. Help."

"Mister Coif, is that you?"

That's strange. How does he know my name?

"Al Coif, are you in there?"

Must be somebody who knows me.

Then the voice was right next to the car.

"Al Coif? It's Officer Walker. Can you hear me?"

"Yes. Yes. I'm in here."

"Are you hurt?"

"Yeah, I'm hurt bad. *Real* bad."

"Okay, just sit tight. We'll get you out as fast as we can."

"Please help me. Please."

Al swiveled his head left, then right, then back again, straining to see the source of the voice. Then, through the windshield, he saw someone standing in front of the Datsun waving his arms. It was a cop. Considering his predicament, he didn't care who it was; he just wanted someone to get him out of the car.

"Help me, please," he pleaded. "I'm in a lot of pain."

"Okay, okay. Just sit tight. I'm going to call for help."

"Yes," whispered Al. "Get help. I need help. Please."

"I'm calling it in now."

*   *   *   *   *

By the time a wrecker got to the scene, the rain had nearly stopped, and daylight was fast declining. Bobcat met the driver on the road and directed him to the Datsun down below.

"Do you think you'll be able to keep it from sliding the rest of the way down the hill?" he asked the driver.

"Not sure. It's pretty steep. He's damn sure lucky that tree was there, or he'd be in the water."

"Yeah," agreed Bobcat, "but he might not see it that way, if he's hurt as badly as he says he is."

"Main thing I'm concerned about is this wet ground," the driver said. "I don't know if I can hold my truck in place and still be able to pull that car back onto its tires. It might pull my truck right in after it."

Bobcat studied the terrain and the condition of the ground. "You might be right," he conceded. "Do you know anyone with a bigger rig that might be able to pull this thing out from up there on the road?"

The young driver scratched the scruffy soul patch beneath his tobacco-filled mouth, then spat a mouthful of amber liquid on the ground. "Jim Cantwell over in Binghamton has one that could pull a railroad car, but it'd take him at least an hour or more to get here. But I can give him a call if you want me to."

"Why don't you do that," suggested Bobcat. "But do it fast. I just don't know how much longer this guy can hang on."

A siren blast from the EMS vehicle above signaled that medical help was on the scene. Bobcat scrambled up the hillside, leaving the tow truck driver with the Datsun.

"Just keep talking to him till I get back, okay?" called Bobcat called over his shoulder to the driver. "I'll be right back."

Chapter 46

Montana

Although Shorty was familiar with the Triple Delight Ranch, he'd never actually been there before. He had no idea how big the spread was, nor how far it might be to the ranch house servicing it. He hopped down from the pickup, and started walking down the rutted dirt road. Small rocks and bits of gravel dug into his unprotected feet, causing him to wince with pain.

It didn't really matter how far it was, he reasoned, because he had to get there and that was that. Bruises and cuts on his feet were the least of his concerns. Getting to that ranch house was all that mattered. His very survival this night depended upon it.

As he walked, he reflected upon his captivity. He really hadn't been abused or harmed; that much was certain. In fact, other than being shackled, he'd pretty much been treated like a guest. The food had been adequate and, owing to the radio he'd been given by Ronald, he'd never felt completely isolated. He'd actually become quite fond of Ronald, and hoped he hadn't injured him during his escape.

Now that he was free, Shorty could understand how kidnap victims often developed symptoms of the "Stockholm Syndrome," made famous when Patty Hearst, the newspaper heiress taken by the Symbionese Liberation Army, used it as an unsuccessful defense to explain her part in a series of bank robberies back in the mid seventies.

Right now, however, Shorty had no such delusions, and little doubt that he would be killed if his captors were successful in tracking him down before he could get help.

* * * * *

As soon as Matt and Chris arrived at the site of the two trailers, it was apparent that something was awry. All the lights were on in both units, and there were no vehicles present.

"What do we do now?" Chris asked.

Matt frowned. "I don't know. I guess we could sit here until somebody comes back . . . but then what?"

"I suppose we don't have a lot of options. And, besides, we don't even know if these people have Shorty."

Matt got out of the car. "I'm going to find out," he declared.

"I'll come with you," Chris assured him.

The two men exited the rental car and started toward the doublewide. As they walked, Matt reflexively patted the Sneaky Pete holster on his belt. Its trademark design made it appear that he was carrying a cell phone rather than a gun. "Sure glad I've got my Glock," he whispered.

Chris smiled and checked his own concealed firearm, located behind his back in its own holster. "That makes two of us," he agreed.

The front door to the doublewide was ajar, but Matt rang the bell, just the same. After three rings failed to yield a response, he pushed through the open doorway and stepped inside.

Because the police had not been contacted, Chris and Matt were not acting in an official law enforcement capacity. In fact, their involvement was essentially that of private investigators, engaged by a private citizen. They didn't require warrants, and weren't limited much in what they could do to unearth evidence. Everything they did was pretty much relegated to that shadowy netherworld between police and private citizen.

"Anybody here?" Matt called.

No answer.

"Come on," he said, "let's look around, see if there's any indication that Shorty's been here."

"Domino's Pizza," said Chris in a loud voice. "Anybody home?"

"Domino's Pizza?" Matt queried his former partner.

Chris smiled. "Why not?"

Matt shrugged his shoulders.

The first two bedrooms were typical trailer fare. Windows bare of curtains, beds unmade, clothing and trash strewn about. A general mess.

The third bedroom was different. There was a shade on the only window, but there was no clothing, nor any refuse at all. The only thing out of place was a roll of duct tape lying on top of the small dresser in the corner of the room. Matt pointed at it, and Chris nodded. "Could be," he whispered. Duct tape was often used in abductions to prevent captives from seeing—and, later, identifying—their captors, and to prevent them from calling for help. Finding it there was both good and bad news. Good, because it probably indicated a crime had taken place. Bad, for the same reason.

A thorough canvass of the dwelling yielded nothing more of value.

"Let's check the trailer out back," suggested Chris.

"Good idea."

The second trailer was much smaller, and in direct contrast to the one out front. Everything was neat and in pristine condition.

"Check all the drawers and closets out here," suggested Matt. "I'll check the bedroom in the back."

Chris began opening—and closing—all the drawers and small closet compartments. If there were anything relative to a crime there, he couldn't find it.

"Bingo!" shouted Matt from the rear of the trailer.

Chris hurried back to find his partner.

"Pay dirt," announced Matt. He was holding a crumpled piece of paper in his hand.

"What is it?"

"See for yourself." Matt handed the piece of paper to his partner. "Go ahead, read it."

"To whom it may concern," Chris read aloud. "I need more time. Please don't hurt Shorty. Here's five thousand dollars . . . Son . . . Of . . . A . . . Bitch! This is it!"

"Like I said," Matt agreed. "It's all we need. If that isn't probable cause I don't know what is. Now we can call the State Police. Have you got your cell phone?"

"Shit, no. I left it back at the ranch. I doubt it would do any good out here, anyway."

"Never mind," Matt said. I saw a wall phone in the kitchen. We can use that."

"I just hope we're not too late," whispered Chris.

"You and me both."

Chapter 47

Roscoe, NY

The crew attached to the EMS vehicle quickly got the driver's side door of the Datsun open, and one of the EMTs crawled inside and was now working diligently to save Al Coif's life.

"Do you think he's going to make it?" Bobcat inquired.

"Hard to say," whispered one of the attendants. "Depends on how long he's been down here."

"Going on two days," replied Bobcat.

The other EMS tech was busy inserting an IV line into the patient's arm, hoping to counterbalance the effects of dehydration with a saline drip. "His pulse is getting stronger," he called back over his shoulder. I think there's a reasonable chance he's going to be okay."

"That depends on your definition of okay," Bobcat whispered.

"How'd he end up here, anyway? Were you chasing him?"

"No, no. I think he's the one responsible for a bunch of barn fires that've been set lately. Night before last, I caught him at the scene of another one, over on DuCoff Road, but he got away . . ."

"Oh."

Bobcat realized how what he had just said might be misconstrued, so he explained further. "He was dead drunk when I got there, lying on the ground. He couldn't even tell me whether or not there was anybody inside the barn, so I went inside to check."

"And *was* there anybody inside?"

"Yeah, as a matter of fact there was. I had to pull the guy out, and, while I was giving him CPR, that's when this fellow managed to get back to his car and escape. I think he just lost control — you know, because he was drunk — and that's how he ended up down here."

"Makes sense to me," conceded the attendant. "I saw the skid marks.

Bobcat just hoped it would make sense to Matt when he got a chance to tell him about it.

An hour or so later, the wrecker arrived from Binghamton, and within a short time, a long, steel cable had been attached to the Datsun by a hook. Rather than risking more injury to Al Coif, they decided not to remove him from the vehicle until it had been righted and pulled up the hill to the road.

Once that had been accomplished, and the vehicle sat on flat ground, they managed to extricate the now unconscious man from the car and lay him on the ground, covering him with a space blanket until they could load him aboard the ambulance. Then, accompanied by Bobcat in his Pathfinder, he was transported to the hospital over in Monticello. The hospital staff was apprised of Al's legal difficulties, and Bobcat transferred custody of his prisoner to the local authorities. He wasn't concerned about Al escaping, but rather whether or not he would survive the night.

* * * * *

Nancy Cooper answered the phone at headquarters, "Roscoe Police Department. How may I direct your call?"

"It's Bobcat. Is Rick around?"

"Uh huh. Want me to put him on?"

"Please."

"Okay. Hang on a second."

Rick came on the line a few minutes later. "What's up, Bobcat?"

"I'm just leaving the hospital over in Monticello and—"

"Hospital? What are you doing over there? Are you okay?"

"Yeah, yeah, I'm fine. I'm just heading back to Roscoe now. I had to drop off my prisoner."

"What prisoner?"

"The guy who set the barn fires."

"You *found* him?"

"I think so. He was trapped inside a wrecked car over on Route Two Oh Six, by the reservoir. I think we've finally got our man."

"Really?"

"Uh huh. I traced that license plate I recorded the other night at the fire over on DuCoff Road and it came back to an Al Coif on Elm Hollow Road, out past Kuttner's place."

"Al Coif? Are you shitting me?"

"No, why?"

"I *know* Al Coif."

"You do?"

"Well, not exactly, but I've known *of* him for years.
Never actually met the guy. Kind of an oddball, they say.
He's Charlie Coif's son. The old man was killed by a
hunter when Al was just a kid. Poor bastard survived
Vietnam and all that shit, then comes home and takes a
ricocheted bullet to the head from a deer hunter's rifle.
Kills him on the spot. They say Al was never the same
after he lost his father."

"No wonder he sets fires."

"So what kind of shape is he in?" Rick inquired.

"Pretty bad. It's a long story. He might not make it."

"What happened?"

"Like I said. It's a long story."

"Well, I'll be here all afternoon."

"Okay. I'll be down in a little while. I'll fill you in
then."

". . . and that's how I burned my hand. Anyway, we
should know in a day or so whether or not he's going to
make it."

Bobcat was holding court at headquarters, explaining
all the intricacies of how he corralled Al Coif to Rick and
Nancy.

"That's some story," Rick acknowledged. "And you're
pretty sure he's the one responsible?"

"No doubt about it. You said you took tire impressions at the fire over in Treadwell, right?"

"Yep."

"Ten to one they'll match those off of Coif's car."

"What kind of vehicle is it?" Rick asked.

"Datsun. Old one. An eighty four, I think."

"That fits," Rick said. "

Bobcat smiled.

"Kind of makes it all worthwhile, doesn't it?" Rick said.

"What?"

Rick pointed at the bandage on Bobcat's right hand. "That."

"Oh . . . well . . . yeah, I guess."

"Matt'll be glad to hear that barn burning situation has been taken care of. Probably get Harold off his case, too."

"Oh fuck Harold," Bobcat said.

"I'll just pretend I didn't hear that," said Nancy with a smile.

"Hear what?" Bobcat said.

"Yeah," agreed Rick. "I didn't hear anything."

"Men," sighed Nancy.

Chapter 48

Montana

Matt punched in the standard three digits used to call emergency services and waited for a reply.

"Nine, One, One. What is your emergency?" The voice was calm and collected, and belonged to a woman.

"This is Chief Matt Davis. I'm here from New York investigating a kidnapping. I need to speak with whoever's in charge."

"Are you a private investigator, sir?"

"No, not exactly. I'm here helping a friend. His ranch foreman has been kidnapped and we were asked to help find him. Is there a police officer I can speak to?"

"Well, sir, I can have someone —"

"Look, I don't have much time," Matt interrupted. He tried hard to hide his impatience. "I need to speak with a police officer right away! *Please.*"

"Just a moment, sir . . ."

A few minutes later, Matt heard a man's voice come on the line. "This is Sergeant Coleman. How can I help you?"

"I'm Chief Matt Davis of the Roscoe, New York, police department," Matt replied. He repeated everything he had told the emergency operator, filling in as much detail as he could, and repeated his "time is of the essence" message.

After explaining the details of the situation further, and providing the officer with more clarification of his and Chris's involvement, Matt got the response he needed to hear.

"How can we help, Chief?"

"I need you to send as many men as possible to this location," Matt commanded the officer. "You do have a fix on our ten-twenty, right?"

"Yessir, we've got you at . . ."

The officer gave Matt the address associated with the landline on which Matt was speaking. "Don't do anything," ordered Sergeant Coleman. "Just sit tight, and we'll have someone on site in twenty minutes."

"I'll be here," Matt assured him. "We're not going anywhere."

* * * * *

Shorty had been walking less than ten minutes when he heard the noise from an approaching vehicle in the distance. He picked up his pace, and was surprised at how stiff his legs were. "Shit," he murmured. "I sure hope that ranch house isn't much further." Apparently, being cooped up on a bed for almost a week had taken its toll on his muscles, because he could feel both calves beginning to cramp.

Suddenly, the terrain in front of him was illuminated brightly, and Shorty wheeled around, only to be blinded by the headlights of a Jeep, which was bearing down on him at a frightening pace. Before he could react, the vehicle skidded to a stop, throwing up a cloud of dust as its wheels fought for purchase on the dirt road. Two men jumped out and came at him from either side. It didn't take them long to subdue him. In less than a minute, his hands were bound behind him with duct tape. Then, they placed tape across his eyes and mouth, and wrestled him inside the Jeep, pushing him down on the floor behind the two, front bucket seats.

"Nice try, white man," said the older of the two men. He had a rifle trained in Shorty's direction. "Too bad you ran out of gas, huh?"

Shorty recognized his voice as that of Injun Four. He had already seen Ronald back at the trailer when he'd escaped.

"Just stay quiet and don't try any funny business," Walter ordered, as he got into the Jeep. He handed the weapon to the younger man. "If he tries anything, shoot him."

"Whatever you say, Walter."

In spite of his words of agreement, Shorty sensed the younger man's heart wasn't in them. If he played his cards right, Shorty still might stand a chance with the young Indian. He wasn't so sure about the other man, however. He relaxed and stayed quiet as he'd been told. He needed to conserve his energy. Walter turned the Jeep around and started back up the dirt road toward the highway.

In a few minutes, the Jeep ground to a halt. Shorty guessed they'd arrived at the spot where he'd abandoned the pickup truck. He was right.

"What're we gonna do about the truck, Walter?" inquired Ronald. "We can't leave it here."

"There's a gas can in the back of the Jeep," Walter replied. "Get it out and pour it into the tank of my pickup, and as soon as you get her running, meet me back at the trailer. I'll take this son of a bitch with me now. So, hurry!"

Shorty heard Ronald exit the Jeep, and a few seconds later, he heard the young Indian retrieve the gas can from the back of the vehicle. Now, Shorty and Walter were alone. The Jeep lurched forward and Shorty began to pray. It wasn't much, but it was all he could do.

God helped those who helped themselves, he thought.

Lord knows I can use all the help I can get.

Chapter 49

When the state police arrived at the site of the two trailers, Matt and Chris met them right away, showed them their credentials, and explained the situation. There were three cruisers, but the first trooper they talked to assured them that more were on the way. Matt suggested they turn off their lights, and asked that any other responding units do likewise.

"I have no idea where they are," Matt informed the officer, referring to the kidnappers. "But I would suggest that we keep a low profile, and wait to see if they come back. As far as I know, they have no idea that we're on to them . . . but I could be wrong."

"So there's no one inside, I take it?"

"Nope. This is exactly how we found things when we got here. It could be that someone tipped them off or—"

"What if you fellows position yourselves at the entrance to the property?" suggested the trooper. "We'll place our vehicles in the rear of the last trailer. That way, when they come back, you can block their exit out front there, and we'll have them surrounded."

"What if they don't come back?" asked Chris.

"Let's cross that bridge when we come to it," responded the trooper.

Matt looked from Chris to the trooper. "So I guess all we can do is just wait . . ."

"I'm afraid so."

Chris tapped his foot nervously on the ground. "How about we run a check for vehicles registered to this address?" he suggested. "That way, we can put out a BOLO."

The trooper appeared somewhat annoyed and quipped, "Don't worry, we've got this."

"Right," Chris allowed. "Didn't mean to step on anybody's toes. Uh, have you already *got* that information?"

"We're working on it," replied the trooper through tight lips. "Don't worry, we'll have it shortly."

"Right," Matt agreed. "Okay then, I guess we'll go get into position. If we need you, we'll beep the horn three times. Okay?"

"Whatever," said the trooper.

"Man," whispered Chris, "we sure pissed *him* off, huh?"

Matt smiled and headed toward the rental car.

* * * * *

When Jimmy and Henry arrived back at the previously closed intersection, the barricades were gone and everything appeared back to normal.

"I guess everything's cool," remarked Henry.

"Yeah. Guess so," agreed Jimmy.

"I don't want to even think about what Walter's gonna say," complained Henry. "When he finds out there's a chance that cops are looking for us, he's gonna want one of us to off that foreman, I just know it—well it *ain't* gonna be me."

"Oh, stop you're bitchin', dude. Nobody's killing anybody. I told you already. We'll just take off. That's all. You'll see."

Henry swung the pickup off the main highway and onto the narrow dirt road leading to the property containing the trailers. He hadn't gone more than a couple of hundred yards when he realized they weren't alone. He had just passed an SUV sitting off to the left with its lights out. Henry went to shift the transmission into reverse, but before he could back up, the vehicle had pulled in behind him and blocked his path.

"Shut your engine off and step out of the vehicle, hands on top of your heads!" he heard someone shout.

"Oh shit," whispered Jimmy. "What are we gonna do?"

Chris and Matt had exited the rental vehicle, and each had his gun drawn. They approached the pickup cautiously, Matt on the driver's side to the left, with Chris on the right.

"Do like they told us," Henry ordered Jimmy.

"Turn off the engine," commanded Matt. "Step out of the vehicle, very slowly. Put your hands on top of your heads. Now!"

"Okay, okay!" shouted Henry through the open window of the pickup. "We're coming out." He reached over and turned off the ignition. "Get out, Jimmy," he said.

Jimmy slowly opened the passenger side door and exited the pickup.

Chris motioned him toward the rental vehicle with his gun. "Put your hands on top of the vehicle and spread your legs."

He quickly frisked the young Indian.

"Okay," he commanded, "get in the back seat."

Jimmy opened the door and climbed inside. Chris moved quickly to the driver's side door and opened it. He reached inside and beeped the horn three times. Almost immediately he heard an engine start in the distance, and he knew help was on the way.

"Don't move!" Chris ordered.

He slammed the door and, using the electronic key control, locked all four of the SUV's doors.

Matt, in the meantime, had removed Henry from the pickup and had him spread-eagled against the tailgate of the truck.

"Nice work, partner," Chris said. "The troopers are on the way."

"Great."

"Kind of feels like the good old days, doesn't it?"

"Yeah," agreed Matt, "except we're a lot older. A *lot* older."

Chris noticed that Matt's hands were shaking ever so slightly.

"Don't worry, partner," Chris assured Matt. "We've got this."

Five minutes later, both Indians had been read their Miranda rights and were in handcuffs in the rear of one of the cruisers. Matt opened the front passenger side door and leaned inside. "Where's Shorty?" he asked.

"Don't know what you're talking about," replied Henry.

"Have it your way," Matt responded. "We know you took him. It's just a matter of time until we find your buddies."

*   *   *   *   *

When Walter pulled the Jeep onto the dirt road leading to the trailers, he couldn't help thinking of how close they'd come to disaster. But now, with Shorty safely recaptured, things were looking up again. They'd have to be more careful in the future, of course, but there wasn't any reason they couldn't move ahead with their plans. He could almost feel the money in his pockets.

"Hey, White Man," he called back to Shorty, "How much money do you think you're worth to that boss of yours?"

Shorty couldn't answer, of course, since his mouth was taped shut, so Walter answered for him. "Probably at least a hundred grand, that's what I think."

He chuckled and then he almost choked when he passed the car parked off to the side of the road in the shadows.

"What the—"

Before he could react, the vehicle had him boxed in from behind, and he knew it was all over. Within minutes, he had joined his fellow Indians in custody. Ten minutes later, Ronald made it a foursome.

Chapter 50

Clint Davidson shook his head in disbelief. He and Shorty were seated at the table in his large country-style kitchen, along with their neighbor, Ralph, and the two New York detectives. From the moment he had discovered his foreman missing, he had never given up hope that Shorty would be found, but as the days had passed, he had to admit his hopes for an acceptable resolution had grown dimmer and dimmer.

"I can't believe it," he conceded. "I had pretty much given up on you fellers." He smiled warmly in the direction of Matt and Chris. "I guess Ralph knew what he was doing when he called you boys for help."

"I guess I did," said Ralph with a wink.

"Well," Clint said, "I can't thank you boys enough. I just wish there was some way I could repay you for all you've done." Then he flashed them a huge smile. "Oh, yeah," Clint informed them, "I *did* manage to get some of that beer you fellers like with that funny sounding name that Ralph told me about."

Clint went over to the refrigerator and extracted a twelve-pack of Yuengling Lager, and plopped it down on the table. "How *do* you pronounce that anyhow?"

Matt and Chris looked at each other and grinned.

"Yingling!" they replied in unison.

Clint broke open the carton and passed a bottle to each of the men. Shorty opened his bottle and raised it in the air. "I think it's me who ought to be most thankful," he allowed. "I only hope there's a place in hell for anybody like those fellers that killed Tyrus."

Clint raised his bottle, "To Tyrus," he said.

"And to Matt and Chris!" Ralph chimed in.

"Here, here," said Clint.

"Here, here," Shorty echoed.

Everyone drained their beers and Clint passed around another round of bottles. Spirits were high, and there was a feeling of well being that bordered on hysteria. And who could blame them.

"So, Matt," Clint inquired, "What's going to happen to those boys?"

"Well, it depends. Most of the money has been recovered, so there's a good chance they could plead a grand larceny charge down to something more manageable. And no one was hurt, thank God, so there's that."

"What about Tyrus?" inquired Clint.

"They'll have to be held responsible for your bull's death, of course," replied Matt. "There's the monetary loss of Tyrus' stud services that has an imputed value. That'll be hard to calculate, but again they might be able to find some compromise on that."

"Does anyone know whether those fellers were ever in any kind of trouble before?" asked Clint.

"Not that we know of," replied Chris.

Then it was Shorty's turn to speak.

"I know what they did to Tyrus is unforgivable," he began, "but aside from that, the way they treated me was pretty decent. That fellow, Ronald, seemed like he really didn't want any part of the whole thing. He's the one who got me the radio. Tell the truth, I never felt in any danger."

Clint listened to his foreman with rapt attention.

Shorty continued. "I know they tried to get some money out of you, Clint, but I think the real thing that bothered them the most was not being able to fish and hunt like their ancestors.

"These people have a long history of being denied their rights. They view most white people as intruders. And, in some sense, I can't argue with that. Maybe if we showed them some common decency, there'd be less problems down the road."

"So, what are you saying, Shorty? I should just *forgive* them?"

"No, no. But maybe they could be made to pay you back. Maybe you could lobby for some kind of repayment plan that would permit them to avoid jail time on the condition that if they missed a payment, or got in any other kind of trouble, they'd have to go to prison."

Clint sipped his beer without answering. He seemed to be considering his foreman's words carefully.

"So," said Ralph, "you boys have one more day here in Montana. Any plans for your *last day*?"

Matt and Chris looked at one another and smiled.

"Okay, okay," laughed Chris. "I can't speak for him, but I think I know what Matt would like to do."

Matt rolled his eyes.

"Come on," said Chris. "You can tell them."

Matt's face flushed with embarrassment.

"Well?" said Ralph. "How about it?"

"Well . . . it would be nice to be able to spend a day fishing without having to worry about being watched, or having to make believe we were having fun when we weren't," Matt admitted.

"Then that's what it'll be," said Ralph. "And I have the perfect guide."

Everyone turned and looked at Clint.

"Don't look at me," he said.

"I was thinking of Shorty," said Ralph. "He probably knows these waters better than all my guides combined. Hell, he's lived here all his life. How about it, Shorty, want to take these two city slickers fishing tomorrow?"

"It'd be my pleasure."

Chapter 51

Roscoe, NY

Rick Dawley hung up the phone and smiled.

"So," Nancy asked, "is he on his way home?"

"Not yet. Apparently, he and his former partner have some unfinished business."

"It wouldn't have anything to do with fishing, would it?"

"No comment."

"Figured as much."

When Matt arrived back from Montana, Nancy Cooper told him the bad news—about her plans to retire *and* about Frank Kuttner's plans to close his shop. Matt wasn't happy about either.

"Well, all I can say," he told Nancy, "is that you've certainly earned your retirement."

"Well, thank you," she replied.

"I don't know how we'll ever replace you," he confided.

"The same way everybody else replaces anyone else who retires. Run an ad. What's that service they're always advertising on TV? Zip Recruiter dot com? You'll figure it out."

She was right of course, thought Matt. He'd find a new secretary.

But, *no one* would ever could or *should* replace Nancy. Of that, Matt was certain. After all, you didn't just replace a fixture.

When Matt pulled up to Kuttner's Fly Shop, he took a good hard look at both the house out front that Frank lived in and the outbuilding that served as his business venue. Both had seen better days. No doubt Frank would have plenty of time to maintain his property, once he retired.

Matt pulled his Wagoneer over to the side of the driveway, leaving plenty of room for any customers that might pull in. He wanted to hear the news from his friend in person. As he approached the door of the little shop, Kuttner magically appeared—as he always seemed to do— on the front porch of his house.

"Sorry, all out of emergers," he called out.

"What's an emerger?"

"Oh, you know," Kuttner quipped, "they're those ratty looking wet flies that *some* people think can catch trout."

"Well, I wouldn't know anything about that."

Frank walked down the front steps and joined Matt at the entrance to his shop.

"Come on in," Kuttner said, opening the door and standing off to the side.

"Thanks. Don't mind if I do."

When they were seated opposite one another in the little rattan seats Frank kept for visitors, Kuttner spoke.

"Tea?"

"Why not?"

Deadly Ransom: A Matt Davis Mystery

Epilogue

Matt and Chris had a fantastic time on the Beaverhead that final day. True to Ralph Gilly's assessment, Shorty proved to be an outstanding guide. All in all, the two men corralled over two dozen trout, with Matt landing the largest one of all, a male brown that tipped the scales at just under seven pounds.

The flight back from Montana was uneventful, and Chris reluctantly acknowledged that maybe flying wasn't all that bad after all. Perhaps he and Matt could consider another trip in the future. He wouldn't promise, but he would definitely think about it.

Harold made Matt promise that he'd never again leave Roscoe for longer than a weekend. Matt made good on his promise to have Clint Davidson reimburse the town for the added expenditure incurred for the substitute police coverage by the State Police. As of this writing, Nancy has yet to be replaced, but has finalized her plans to visit England.

Val welcomed Matt with open arms, and the two celebrated his return with a well-deserved dinner at Raimondo's, their favorite restaurant. Rumor has it that Matt actually got to enjoy some anchovies on his salad. Val will neither deny or confirm the rumor.

Several months after he returned to Roscoe, Matt got word from Ralph about the disposition of the case against the four Native Americans. Shorty's recommendation was listened to and considered by the local prosecuting attorney for the area, but, in the end, the men were convicted and sentenced — albeit to fairly lenient sentences, with a good possibility of parole. Clint has made plans to make his land available to Native Americans on a limited basis.

Al Coif remained in the hospital for nearly two weeks after his rescue from the wrecked car. The spiral fracture he suffered to his leg would forever keep him from walking without a limp, but the broken ribs and lacerated liver would heal. His jail sentence would keep the community safe for as long as it lasted. His broken psyche, however, would most likely never be repaired.

Oh, and the Monticello newspaper did feature an article about Matt and Chris saving Shorty's life out in Montana, but made no mention at all of Mayor Harold Swenson.

Acknowledgments

As is always the case when writing a novel, there are countless individuals without whose help a book might never be written.

Heartfelt thanks to Chris Freitag, retired police captain and longtime friend, for his continuing support and assistance. Not only has he allowed me to think and act for him as Matt's partner, but has answered every inane procedural question I have asked without once making me feel stupid.

Thank you to Mike Robinson for his cover photo, "Montana Summer Evening." You can see more of his work on his website at: www.tau0.wordpress.com.

Special thanks to former Montana fly fishing guide Greg Lilly. Having Mr. Lilly's experience to draw upon made it possible for me to write the scenes involving the Beaverhead River as if I had actually experienced them for myself.

As usual, for permitting me to "use and abuse" their actual names and their personalities as those of my characters, I am eternally grateful to Nancy Cooper, Rick Dawley, Joyce Hillriegel, Frank Kuttner, Bruce Pfeffer, Dr. George "Pete" Richards, and Robert "Bobcat" Walker.

My gratitude to all my family, friends, and acquaintances (you know who you are) for your unwavering support and encouragement, without which I could never succeed.

Special thanks to Bill Farkas, who volunteered as a Beta reader, whose task was to uncover my mistakes and typographical errors.

My eternal gratitude and love to my wife, Becky, for her unending support, and for reading, critiquing, and listening to my endless middle-of-the-night ramblings. Though it might not always seem so, I trust her completely and value her judgment. She is my muse.

Lastly, a huge group hug to all my faithful readers. I know this book's been quite a while coming, but your continuing support and encouragement has not gone unnoticed. This one is for you!

NOTE: There is an interesting back story concerning the character of Al Coif. One day, while lunching with Jim Krul, the former director of the Catskill Fly Fishing Center and Museum in Livingston Manor, NY, I noticed his license plate read AL COIF. I inquired as to its significance, and he handed me a business card. It showed that the name is actually an acronym for A Loose Confederation Of International Flyfishers. So, my thanks to Jim for allowing me to use the "name" for one of my characters and also for making me an honorary member of ALCOIF.

A Word About Roscoe

The last four books in the Matt Davis Mystery Series, including this one, have been set in the town of Roscoe, NY. Some readers may have wondered whether or not Roscoe is a real place, or just one that I have created for the series. The answer is both. Allow me to explain.

There is the real town of Roscoe, NY, located about two hours north of New York City at Exit 94 of NY State Highway 17, in the lush Catskill Mountains. For as many years as I can remember, it has been known affectionately as Trout Town USA. Today, thanks to a contest held in 2012 by the World Fishing Network, this little town whose resident population is a mere 600 has been voted the Ultimate Fishing Town USA, after receiving 267,435 votes and narrowly edging out much larger cities such as Denver, San Diego, and Key West. One thing is certain, however. This Roscoe, with its wonderful trout-filled waters, comforting mountains, and friendly people, is a place that is dear to my heart—and most definitely *not* a haven for criminals.

Then, there is the other Roscoe, the one that I alter and configure in whatever manner I see fit to serve the various story lines of my Matt Davis Mystery Series. For instance, Raimondo's Italian Restaurant really does exist (it's both Matt's and my favorite place to eat), but the Roscoe Police Department with its well-defined "headquarters" building does not. Some characters, like Frank and Mary Ellen Kuttner are very real (see the acknowledgments), and others, like the mayor and council, are a figment of my imagination. So what is real and what is not? That, dear reader, is for you to discern.   Good luck and happy reading!

About the Author

Joe Perrone Jr. began writing seriously in 1969 as a sportswriter for the Passaic-Clifton, NJ, *Herald News*. From there he moved on to freelance copywriting for a number of advertising agencies.

His first book was *Gone Fishin' with Kids (How to Take Your Kids Fishing and Still be Friends)*, a non-fiction collaboration with his friend and co-author, Manny Luftglass. The book was published in 1997.

Joe's first two novels were published in 2005: *Escaping Innocence (A Story of Awakening)* is a coming-of-age novel set in the turbulent '60s; *As the Twig is Bent* is a mystery/thriller set in New York City, and launched the highly successful Matt Davis Mystery Series. When it was first published, *As the Twig is Bent* reached the #24 bestseller mark in the Kindle book store.

He followed "Twig" with four other Matt Davis mysteries, including *Opening Day, Twice Bitten, Broken Promises*, and *Deadly Ransom*. Both *Opening Day* and *Broken Promises* were awarded the prestigious Indie BRAG Medallion for excellence in independent publishing. In 2009, Joe published his other non-fiction book, *A "Real" Man's Guide to Divorce (First, you bend over and . . .)*, which is exactly what its title implies, with a wry touch of humor.

In 2012, Mr. Perrone founded Escarpment Press, primarily a publishing consulting company offering services to independent authors. Escarpment Press publishes several books each year.

Joe and his wife, Becky, live in the mountains of Western North Carolina with their two calico cats, Cassie and Callie. A former professional guide for ten years, the author enjoys fly fishing, fly tying, cooking, music, and watching movies. He loves to hear from his readers, and welcomes email comments and inquiries via email at: joetheauthor@joeperronejr.com.

Mr. Perrone is active on social media, and can be found on Facebook and Twitter. He also writes a weekly blog at: www.joetheauthor.wordpress.com. His personal website is www.joeperronejr.com, and independent authors can learn more about his publishing consulting firm at: www.escarpmentpress.weebly.com.

Joe is currently at work on a stand-alone thriller entitled *Getting Even!* that is scheduled for release some time in 2021.

www.ingramcontent.com/pod-product-compliance
Lightning Source LLC
Chambersburg PA
CBHW021204250626
47155CB00008B/2662